Career-driven Meghan always thought she would make partner by thirty until a new transfer is brought in to help close a corporate merger, disrupting her plan with motives that have the potential to upend more than just her career.

Meghan's hard work is about to pay off. She always knew she would make partner by thirty. With only a few weeks working on the largest merger of her career left, everything seems to be going to plan. Until she meets the new transfer, Shane. Though he was hired under the guise of helping to secure the deal, Shane's behavior begins to cause Meghan to wonder if he has different motives after all.

Hostile Takeover is a new adult dark romance. This book contains many triggers, including, but not limited to, references to sexual assault, violence, kidnapping, and issues affecting sobriety.

Hostile Takeover
Copyright © 2024 Arabella Ames
ISBN: 978-1-4874-3982-8
Cover art by Martine Jardin

Published by eXtasy Books Inc

Look for us online at:
www.eXtasybooks.com

Hostile Takeover

By

Arabella Ames

Dedication

To Valerie, for reading every story I've ever written. And to Rebecca, who'd read everything before it was good.

Chapter One: Meghan

*F*uck. I'm late. It's probably why I left my apartment wearing the one shirt I own that has a missing button. I smooth down the fabric over my breasts. It's definitely noticeable. I flip down the visor and slide open the mirror. Great, it's very noticeable. I groan and twist around to try to find a better blazer or a scarf in the backseat, but the seatbelt clicks into place. Frustrated, sweating, and now very, very late, I free myself of my restraint and find an ugly cream-colored blazer crumbled beneath the underside of the passenger seat. I bring it to my nose and inhale and thank the universe that it doesn't smell.

I've worked at Morgan & Miller since my time as a summer associate during law school. Environmental law has always been my passion, but big law is how young lawyers actually build power to make change. Mergers and Acquisitions might seem boring to most, but to me, it's how I'll change the world. I've been on the partner track for the last five years, and this year is finally my year. Unfortunately, they're only promoting two junior partners this time. If I don't get it now, I risk death-by-senior-associate, and no one wants that.

The deal I'm working on now should secure my future. If I can secure the deal, that is. Big clients are always a big risk. Egos can quickly upend a contract negotiation that seems perfect. But with a tight deadline, I need one more major client to prove my worth. And the Phoenix deal is the biggest client I've been given point on so far.

I don't know if I believe in fate, but if I did, this would be it. I smooth the collar of my blazer. It feels like my entire life has been building to this very moment, this exact week. I can almost feel the future I've always dreamed of within my grasp. All my hard work, all the long nights working, all the weekends lost to my career, it's all about to pay off. And once I'm a partner, I can really make a difference.

As long as Michele Morgan doesn't see me half-dressed and ten minutes late in the hallway.

The elevator is on my side today, and there's a few people away from their desks. I make it to my small office with little incriminating interaction. I even have just enough time to set up my laptop and take a sip of my coffee when I hear footsteps.

"Good morning, Meghan," Michele says.

"Good morning," I say. I button my blazer while still trying to catch my breath.

"The new transfer will be down shortly. He's just wrapping up paperwork with HR."

"Oh, right . . . thanks."

"You didn't forget, right?" Her eyebrows raise into her hairline.

"No, of course not. Long night reading contracts. Sorry, just waking up still." I hold up my clear coffee tumbler as proof.

"Okay, well . . . maybe drink it all before he gets here or something. You seem off. We received fifteen more boxes from Phoenix's firm this morning, and there's a client meeting at noon. You'll have to get him up to speed quickly and put him to work." She taps her hand on my desk and offers me a tight smile that suggests she's already annoyed and unwilling to accept anything less than perfection.

"Will do," I say. I watch for her to turn the corner before I hurry off to print copies of the documents I need before this guy gets here.

It's not that I forgot. I definitely remember the conversation where Michele offered me point and explained that I'd get help with whatever I needed. It's exciting to prove myself and mentor others—another sign that becoming a partner is deserved and that my career is working out. It's just that I vaguely remember the new guy's name and certainly didn't remember to have Clara mark his start date in my calendar.

As usual, Clara's missing, and there's no paralegal to be found. Luckily, the printer isn't busy, and I'm able to make everything I need without waiting. Incompetence would be a poor first impression, and the client is coming in today. To be put in M & A then to help with a high-profile deal right away? This guy is probably some legacy whose parents got him into *Harvard*, who will be hyper-critical of me if I show up unprepared. I love my law firm, but that doesn't change the fact that no one can be trusted, and everyone's opinion matters. If I'm anything less than the best, someone will find out, and I'll be passed over. Transfer or not, everyone is a threat, and no one can be underestimated.

I drop the stack of papers as I round the corner, carrying too much and all at once. I'm impatient in nearly everything I do. I stare at the mess, considering leaving it on the floor and finding a paralegal to take pity on me. If this is how my day is starting, I'm not so sure my patience will survive through lunch.

"Er, I can come back later," a man says.

I bend down to scoop up the scattered papers and nearly drop them again when I stand straight and turn around to see who's speaking.

The man is handsome. Tall, maybe a foot taller than me. His sharp brown eyes peer down at me like he can see through my skin. I should look away but can't. I swallow my nerves.

Everything about him is harsh. Maybe it's his height, the

way he towers over me, that brings out a sharp hollowness to his face. It casts a menacing shadow across his defined cheekbones. His full lips are pursed slightly, almost in disapproval. And his jawline clenches as he assesses my too-long stare.

He glares at me for a moment before breaking the tension. "I'm Shane," he says. He holds out his hand for me to shake, and I process the gesture a few seconds too slowly to feel normal. "The transfer."

"Meghan," I say roughly. I shift the papers to shake his hand, and my already simmering agitation turns to full-blown annoyance as his large fingers easily overpower mine to dominate the handshake. I fucking hate men. I don't let go until he does, causing him to smirk as if he's won some invisible power struggle. I want to stare him down. Intimidate him the way he's tried to intimidate me. But he's so tall and so close to me that I have to take a half step backward just to be able to look him in the eyes.

"Do you, um, need me to come back later?" He looks me up and down as if assessing me. "You seem . . . disheveled." The smirk is back.

Fuck this guy. His first impression of me will be my incompetence. I shouldn't have stayed up so late reading when I knew I had early meetings today. I just wanted to get this done. There're only so many weeks I can live teetering on the edge of success and failure before I break. If I'm going to make partner, I need to be more resilient. I can't be showing up late, unprepared.

My annoyance with myself is short-lived as his gaze pauses on my chest, then darts away only when caught. *What the fuck?* First, the weird power-hungry handshake, and now this. I don't have time to handle misogyny on top of everything else. At least the asshole has the decency to look ashamed. *Fucking pervert.* Just because he's a man and has smoldering eyes and confidence doesn't give him the right to sexualize me. I'm essentially his boss for the next six weeks, not his fucking date.

Then I see the smugness slip away as a blush creeps across his face, and I remember my broken button and quickly hug the papers over my chest. *Shit*. Okay, so maybe he's not a pervert. It's me. He's going to think I'm trying to seduce him.

"I'm sorry," I start to explain. The last impression I want to give is unprofessional. "I got dressed in the dark, and I, I . . . the button broke. I don't usually look like this." I sound less competent the longer I talk.

"It's all right. I didn't, um, could we, uh, just start over." He laughs nervously and runs a hand through his dark hair, and it's at that moment I realize he's not just sort of attractive. He's beautiful.

My stomach clenches. It's my turn to blush. *Fuck*, of course I'm awkward around the first hot guy at the firm. This is why my relationships never work out. It's like my brain can't process how a man can be both a person and have potential. People, I can navigate. I've perfected pretending. Potential scares the shit out of me. Best-case scenario, potential can lead to disappointment. Worst-case, potential can hurt. A lot.

"Hi, I'm Shane. I'm the new guy. And you must be Meghan?" He holds out his hand again and smiles. He feels more approachable when he smiles. "I'm excited to be here. I'm lucky to work under you. I've heard great things." His face transforms into something warm and comforting, and I can't help but return the gesture. This time, his fingers are gentle, and his hold on my hand feels more like a caress.

A shiver runs down my spine at his touch, but again, I'm the last to pull away, this time for an entirely different reason.

"It's nice to meet you, Shane," I say, even though I'm not sure I should mean it.

We spend the rest of the morning together. I show him around the office, and to his credit, his personality improves.

He's attentive. Polite. Deferential. When I give him my list of work I need completed before the client meeting at noon, he does it by eleven and asks for more. I almost start to like him.

Almost.

At first, I think I'm happy to have someone new in the office I can work with. I don't have a lot of friends outside of work. It takes up so much of my life it's hard to do anything else. Or talk about anything else, for that matter. Even when I leave this place, it's all I think about. But after the meeting, I find myself peering out the office glass just to see him. He's so handsome, and it's not wrong to look. Most of the time, he's too busy to notice or too caught up in a conversation with another associate. Then sometimes, his gaze finds mine, and he grins. Each time that delight shines over his face, my pulse races.

I shouldn't give in to impulse. Instead of admiring his face or imagining what it'd feel like to press my body into his, I think of all the horrible qualities he must possess. He's a man. He's a handsome man, so he's probably a womanizer. He probably smiles at me, then scans the office for other potential women he can fuck. He probably rates all of us, and I doubt I make his list.

His knuckles rap against my open office door before he walks back in.

"All done, boss. What's next?" he asks. His long legs cross the room to my desk in three easy steps. He pauses next to me, not in front of my desk like I expect, not in a chair where he could wait patiently like I'd prefer. He stands right next to me. So close I can feel the brush of his clothes against mine.

I don't usually like it when people get too close. I swallow. "You're done already?" I ask, but don't look for his response. I keep my gaze carefully in front of me, hoping that if I pretend he's not next to me, he'll fade away.

"I work fast," he says. He shifts his weight from one foot to the other but doesn't step back.

"You can take lunch then," I say, glancing at the time on my watch.

"You wanna come with me? I'm still pretty new here. Maybe you could show me which places are best."

"You're not from here?" I ask that instead of offering to spend more time together. I really should stay focused.

"Nah." He finds something across the room to be interested in, creating a bit of space for me to relax.

"Where did you go to law school?" Now that he's feet away, I look up. He slips his hands into his pockets and paces around, moving from one framed diploma to the next.

"Yale."

I roll my eyes. Of course he went to Yale. I bet his parents went to Yale, too. That's how he got transferred here. His parents are definitely some big shots. I hate nepotism.

"You?" he asks, turning to me.

"University of Chicago."

"So why Morgan & Miller?"

I shrug. "I wanted to work in corporate law that didn't bore me to death without completely losing my soul in the process."

"Well . . ." He walks back over and takes a seat. He crosses an ankle against his knee, one arm draped over his leg. "Corporate law, check. Not bored to death, check. How's the soul?"

I laugh despite myself, and he smiles. "The soul is all right, still intact, though I guess the jury is out on whether that'll last long term." I chew on my lip. My own humor dies out as I realize just how true those words ring. I shift uncomfortably in my chair. I don't want to dwell on that too long, not here, not in front of someone I barely know.

I clear my throat. "There's a great place down the block. A lot of us go there for lunch."

"All right, let's go." He claps his hands as he stands and steps toward the door.

I shake my head. "Thank you for the offer. But I need to wrap this up. Next time, though." I look up to offer him a consolatory smile but stop short. He watches me. His gaze catches on my mouth as my nerves cause me to take my bottom lip between my teeth once more.

I can feel the tension build between us. Its magnetic energy is palpable, begging me to go to his side so we can be closer.

"Is there anything I can bring back for you?" His words cut through the uncertainty I feel.

I blink and try to brush it off. "Just a coffee," I say. "Dark roast if they have it, black."

Chapter Two: Shane

"Is there another associate I can work with?" I ask. I have to keep my hands firmly in my pockets to stop from showing signs of frustration. It won't help my case if I appear agitated. Women tend to view male aggression as a sign of weakness. Michele would be more likely to send me off to the filing room than accommodate my urgent need if I came in here demanding things on my second day.

"Is there something wrong with Meghan?" she asks. Her face remains smooth, calm, if not a tiny bit confused. No sign of concern or fear.

I exhale. "Meghan is perfect." The words nearly choke me. Surely, there's another attorney on this case I can work with. Someone else with leverage who doesn't look up at me with sweet bright eyes and soft full lips. She's so fucking cute it hurts. I squeeze my hands into fists and release them. I can't afford any distractions. I can't allow myself to care for an assignment.

I went home last night and only thought of her. The way she pushed her auburn hair behind her ears. The way her glasses slipped down her nose and her neck strained to meet my eyes. My father must have known he'd be testing my loyalty, assigning me to her. I tried telling myself that she's like any other person. But there's something about her that I can't shake. I know if I see her again today, I'll break.

I need to get rid of her. I'm sure that I can rush through the Phoenix deal without having to work one-on-one with her directly, especially if there's another attorney who I can bide my time with. "They're almost to due diligence. I was just wondering if there was another client I could work with, establish better relationships with from the beginning." I make a point to fidget and scratch the back of my neck. If I look uncomfortable, she might take pity on me.

Michele considers me for a moment before speaking. "Associates typically don't get to make requests. Especially new ones." Her lips thin into a disapproving line.

I cross the room and take the seat in front of her desk, bringing us closer to eye level. "I know, and I apologize." I lean forward slightly, chin down, with my hands folded in my lap. I look at her and hold her gaze for a few seconds before looking away. I know it's working when I hear the catch of her breath. "But if there was any chance I could expand my experience, my relationships, I just know it would help me contribute more."

I look back at her, counting to three before looking down at her lips, then back up, forcing my face into a timid smile.

"Shane," she says. Her tone is serious, but I can hear the undertones of flirtation.

And just like that, I've won.

It's a delicate balance, using sexual tension as a tool of manipulation in the workplace. But it's a skill I've mastered, among others. My charm and discretion have become my father's secret weapons. Far more useful to him than my brief, rebellious military career or my half-hearted attempts at keeping the family law firm's legacy alive. I've gone from the worst mistake to my father's greatest asset in all of three years.

If I keep this up, I might even become the favorite son, maybe even put back into the will.

"I'm not sure there's someone working on anything relevant." Michele tears her eyes away from my face and quickly scans her computer. She clicks her mouse. "I suppose I could find something for you. Give me time. It does help that you're a lateral transfer. We won't have to worry about billable hours for a few weeks while you adjust to the office." She clicks through several things before looking back up at me. Her eyes widen slightly as she meets my gaze. "Or if you bring in your own client, we can talk about your future here more often."

"I would be so grateful." I reach my hand out and set it on her desk, leaning forward, my fingers inches away from her own. "Really, it would mean so much to me. I'd do anything."

"Okay, well." She straightens her shoulders slightly and blinks away the lustful fog I see building behind her eyes. "Let me just, let me just rearrange some things, and I'll see what I can do." She clears her throat, turning her attention back to her screen. "I'll try my best."

There's nerves and excitement there. I see it in her movements, hear it in her words, and the way she tucks the dark strands of hair behind her ears as she glances up at me from behind her glasses. Michele is pretty. *Powerful.* A Morgan of Morgan & Miller. But successful women love a certain type of man. With her slender hands ring free, I can read her thoughts without trying. She's going out of her way to accommodate me because she's imagining our possibilities. She's thinking of the opportunity that helping me might provide.

I almost feel guilty playing into her fantasies. Almost. A part of me wonders if she'll even realize it was me when the deal goes through, but their client ends up unhappy. I don't think I'll be around long enough to ask.

"I can take a look at some things and finalize a plan for you by the end of this week?"

The end of the week is too long. That's three more days with Meghan. My knee starts to jiggle with frustration before I catch myself. I close my eyes and count down from five. In order to make this work, I need to stay calm. I can't draw more attention to myself than I have already. I must remain the quiet, handsome associate, and nothing more.

"In the meantime, I can let Meghan know your interests, and perhaps she'll have an idea for what you can do."

"No, that's all right," I say in a rush. "I'd hate to inconvenience her on my behalf." And I'd hate to be near her a second longer than absolutely necessary, I think to myself. I can't risk being distracted again. My father won't always be there to bail me out of my failures. He made sure to make that point clear when he reluctantly helped me clear my record at the start. But I'm smarter now. Whether he likes it or not, the military taught me a lot. I know how to execute a plan and hide any evidence.

I have three weeks at most. In and out. It's more than enough time. I can't afford to have something fuck this up.

"Don't be silly." She waves away my concern. "Meghan is a workhorse. She'd be more than happy to put you somewhere she needs that also benefits you." Her fingers tap away at her phone, and she smiles. "Done. Meghan will guide you in the meantime, and we can circle back later next week."

I grind my teeth together, forcing my lips into a tight smile. "Thank you so much for your help." I stand quickly. I need to leave this room.

The hallway doesn't provide the relief I crave. It's like everywhere I go, my head is filled with Meghan. She's not special. I repeat it like it's a mantra. She's just another assignment. One I can't afford to fuck up. There's no guilt inside me to ease. I lost those kinds of emotions long ago. Maybe it was the Army. Maybe it was being raised by my father or by a woman who never wanted to be my mother. Either way, I learned from a young age that if I fail to take what I want, someone else will.

If it's not me on this assignment, it's my brother, or one of my father's people. It's not like the problem disappears if I do. And that gives me the ability to push forward.

Meghan is lucky it's me. Even if I'm not lucky it's her.

Chapter Three: Meghan

It's not even nine in the morning, and Michele has completely upended my plan for my day. I sigh into my coffee. Partner track, I repeat to myself. This is all for making partner. The steam from it fogs my glasses, and I have to take them off to see. *Shane.* I pinch the bridge of my nose and close my eyes. I just know it's his fault. I replay yesterday in my mind. Nothing goes smoothly when it comes to my career. I thought that taking point while also taking on an associate would help me look better when it came time to decide on a partner. Not only am I capable, but now I'm a team player. Then my associate showed up looking like Shane.

I can't stop picturing his face. The cheekbones and full lips. How it felt when he introduced himself and shook my hand the second time. How it felt to sit next to him. The way his knee rested against mine as I showed him what files I needed to review. The way our hands inched closer together throughout the day, until I could feel the heat of his body against my skin.

"Good morning," Shane says.

It makes me jump in my chair. I spill coffee on my white blouse. "Fuck." I stand, setting down my coffee with force, and grab my glasses. "You shouldn't do that," I say. I glare up at him. He stands too close to me. I have to crane my neck to see him fully. "You shouldn't just sneak up on people." I place my hands on my hips. "Look what you've done. I've got a meeting with our client today."

His mouth twitches in amusement. His bottom lip curves

up to one side in a way that makes me feel like his opponent again. "It's not my fault you're blind and couldn't see me coming."

"Ha. Ha. You're so funny, Shane. A glasses joke. I've never heard that before." I walk by him, not bothering to avoid his body. I angle my shoulder into his ribs as I shove past and hurry toward the restroom. I refuse to show any sign of his effect on me. But I'll certainly be instructing Clara not to let him in my office without warning.

The automatic lights blink on as soon as I enter the restroom. The white marble magnifies the brightness of the room. I groan. The stain is huge. The width of the far wall by the sink is covered by a mirror, and even from this distance, I can see the bleeding brown liquid stretching across the left side of my chest.

Stupid man and his stupid deep voice. I don't usually like men to begin with. But this one especially. He's antagonized me from the moment we met. I hate his stupid face that I can't even see because he's so annoyingly tall. I grab a handle full of paper towels from the dispenser and turn on the water, dabbing my shirt yet somehow making the appearance worse. This is my brand-new silk blouse. I want to scream.

"Need some help?"

I look up to find Shane's reflection in the mirror. Our eyes meet in the glass, his deep brown to my green. He stalks toward me, slowly, stopping to stand right behind me. He towers above me, staring at my reflection in the mirror without blinking.

I can feel his body heat against my skin without touching him. It makes me shiver.

"You can't be in here," I say. I whirl around to face him at the same time he steps closer, and I slam my face into his chest.

His deep laughter rumbles against my cheek as he wraps

his hands around my arms. "Hard day? If you needed a hug, all you had to do was ask."

I step backward out of his grasp. "Don't touch me." I slap away his hands. "What if someone walks in." I glance around, sweeping the room for signs of witnesses. Getting caught is probably the wrong concern. I should be outraged that he's so openly flirtatious. The last thing my career needs is false rumors of a sordid love affair. How cliché to seduce the impressionable transfer. Embarrassment trickles down my neck and makes me sweat. My chance at making partner anywhere would be dead.

"No one will walk in—" he says calmly.

"You can't be in here," I interrupt him. I try to make my voice more stern, but the words come out with less certainty than I intend.

"I can be wherever I want." He steps closer. The sentiment rumbles in my chest. "Besides, I came in here to help you."

I don't know why, but I have this subtle suspicion that Shane doesn't like me. Most of the time, he's all smiles and polite, albeit mischievous, energy. Then sometimes, I catch him out of the corner of my eye and see something entirely different cross his face. Occasionally, that dark edge I suspect even bleeds into his voice.

It clouds my judgment when I can't pin down someone's emotions. Deep down, I'm a people pleaser. It makes me desperate to understand those around me so that I can win them over. It helps me be the best, the favorite. A skill that's come in handy for my career, even in my relationships. But I can't tell with Shane. One minute, I think I've charmed him. The next, I feel as if I've repulsed him in some way.

I tell myself I'm overthinking. Anyone can begin to find eccentricities if they stare long enough. It's not that he likes or doesn't like me. I've obsessed too much in too short of time to interact normally. Besides, Shane doesn't feel like a man I should want to understand. A part of me screams in warning, begging me to stay away. Men are not safe, it reminds me. And the men that can draw a person in are the most dangerous.

"I don't know why you care." I spin back around. I turn on the faucet and do my best to pretend he isn't there, soaking the towel again and dabbing at my top until it's saturated.

"Don't be so stubborn. Let me help." He pulls me by my arms and turns me around to face him, pushing my back into the sink, and trapping me against the counter with his body. I can feel him press into me. The hardness of his body dominates the softness of mine. It's like a bomb is set off in my mind. Coherent thought is eradicated, and all I can feel is the desire I've held dormant within me for so long, begging to be set free.

"Shane." I breathe his name in warning. His large hands hold me firmly still as my heart hammers in my chest. The heat of his body warms me. The smoke and spice smell of his cologne draws me in further. My stomach buzzes with potential, my muscles clenching at the proximity of his hips to mine, at his confidence to touch me and do so with such certainty. And power.

"Shut up and stay still," he says.

My chest heaves up and down—no longer in fear of being caught, but from the way my pulse beats faster at his command. The labor of my breath is the only sound I can hear. I try to soothe myself so he won't notice, but as his eyes flicker from my mouth back to my eyes, it seems I've failed.

Then his brown eyes burn black with something that looks a lot like disgust.

Shit. I do repulse him. I've mistaken his kindness for something more. *Oh god*, it's been too long since I've sex. I'm too obvious. Desperate. The embarrassment cools my desire with shame.

"W-what?" I struggle to speak. I want to play it off, but the words come out trembling with what sounds like loosening control. I'm an idiot. He can tell I'm attracted to him, and he's not attracted to me. I'm so obvious it's pathetic.

Shane's hands grip me harder. His long fingers keep me trapped against him. He looks me up and down in disapproval. "Don't you have a boyfriend?"

"Wh-what? No?" He really can tell I'm attracted to him, and now he thinks I'm also a whore. Or a workplace predator who abuses her power to seduce younger, impressionable men.

"Don't lie to me, Meghan."

The force of his concern draws us closer, and I wonder if he even realizes it. Maybe he's not disgusted by me. There's passion there. I'm not sure for what, but I could easily find out. All it would take to reach up and kiss him is a stretch onto my tiptoes. I wonder if his kiss would be as demanding as his other behavior.

"I'm not in a committed relationship." If I thought my words would ease his concern, I was wrong. His muscles only tighten more, and something like fear crosses his face. It's like cold water to the nerves. I come to my senses, this time for good. I shouldn't like this. Can't like how it feels to be this close. I won't be caught in this position with my reputation compromised.

"Get off me. My dating life is none of your business." For the second time today, I shove away his body with my shoulder.

"Don't be ridiculous," he says. His voice is cruel. "It's not like I care either way."

I make it only a few steps before I'm in Shane's hands once more. It catches me off-guard, and I stumble slightly, my balance held upright by his steady presence.

"I'm not asking you to care," I say, jerking away. Tears

prick hot behind my eyes, and I want to run out of there before the shame really sets in. I should've known better. Men that look like him can't be any good.

"Clearly." He smirks. Sarcasm drips from his tongue. He holds me still and pulls out a *Tide* stick from his pocket. "But I was trying to give you this, weirdo. It'll help with the stain."

I blink up at him, trying to process his kindness but unable to figure out why he chose this moment to care after terrorizing me. He could've offered this in the beginning. Tentatively, I take the stick from his hand and turn back toward the mirror, leaning over the sink to better see. To my surprise, and annoyance, it works pretty well—it might've worked better had I done this immediately. Although the stain has mostly gone, in its place is a large wet patch of fabric that clings to my skin. I look disheveled, just like the first day he met me. My face is red from embarrassment, and my clothing crumbled.

"Here," Shane says. He slips off his blazer and drapes it around my shoulders. "Wear this. No one will see." He rolls back the sleeves of his button-down, revealing a small tattoo above his wrist.

I want to reach out and touch him. Run my nails over his skin, pull his face down to mine, and devour him whole. Instead, I say, "I can't wear this." I shrug it off my shoulders and try to give it back, but he shakes his head and walks toward the door. Leaving me cold in the sudden absence of his body.

"You should really take it." He pauses in the doorway, looking back at me. He nods in my direction. "Cause I can see your piercings. Which means everyone else will, too."

I gape at his retreating figure and look down to see that he's right. *Fuck.* I smooth my shirt before reluctantly slipping my arms through the blazer. It smells like him. I breathe in the fabric and hate myself immediately. *Stupid.* I'm being stupid. He doesn't like me. He likes to taunt me. To push my boundaries and make me react. He doesn't like me as a person, and he certainly doesn't care for me. He went out of his way to make that very clear. So I should steer far, far away from him.

Chapter Four: Shane

I can't pinpoint the moment when distraction turned into outright derailment. That's the annoying part of working with Meghan. She's so beautiful. Her perfect little face. The way she bites her lip before she speaks when she's nervous, and I seem to make her nervous a lot. The way she has to look up at me. *Oh, god.* That fucking look she gets in her eyes when she has to look up at me. It was one thing when I thought she was just another high-powered piece in a corporate game I had to play. But as that innocent façade slips away and her intellectual fight rises up to meet mine, I'm drawn to her even more.

My phone buzzes in my pocket. My father. I can't get away with ignoring him much longer. It's been two days. We're under a tight timeline, so he'll expect an update soon, and certainly not the one I'd be able to provide as of now. What would I say? *Hi, Dad. I've learned nothing except Meghan has really great tits that got even better when I learned they're pierced.* He'd murder me himself. I silence the call. He'll be less angry this way than if I was honest. I'll blame it on a meeting and find some detail to give him later that gets him off my ass for a few more days.

If Michele can't help me, then I'll use today to find a different target. There's someone who's of equal value. Someone who doesn't feel so unpredictable. One of the things I learned in the Army was the importance of self-control. My own reaction can be the difference between success and failure. And I can't exactly control my emotions when Meghan's constantly pulling me in like some bespoke siren bent on bringing me to my knees.

Mmm. I wonder what she would do with me kneeling before her. She practically swooned at my touch yesterday. I can almost hear her tiny squeal as I trap her hips in my hands and run my lips over those soft thighs and bury my face in her sweet cunt.

No.

I pull at my suit pants and try to readjust myself. I can't keep thinking about her. The fantasies have morphed into an obsession. I already have to jerk off before work now just to make it through the day next to her. And that release alone is already not enough.

I pull out my phone to distract myself and text my brother.

Shane — *Coming home next Friday. Dress code is cocktail attire?*

Carson — *Wtf dude*

Carson — *You're an adult. You have to rsvp to this shit.*

Carson — *We don't have a seat for you.*

Shane — *Beige suit then? Perfect.*

Carson — *Abbey will fucking divorce me if you show up like that.*

Carson — *Black-tie affair motherfucker*

Carson — *Jesus Christ*

Carson — *At least don't be late to the ceremony, okay?*

Carson — *And tell Mom you're coming home. Or I will.*

My mother. I groan. I didn't think of that. In my attempt to escape the gravitational pull of Meghan, I've run straight into the turmoil of my parents. I stand up from my desk and pace back and forth, running my hands through my hair to think. My parents are . . . formidable. My father understands me — or maybe accepts me is the more appropriate description. He's at least grown to see value in my strengths. Come to terms with what I have to offer.

My mother, on the other hand. To say I'm a disappointment could not begin to describe our relationship. She may have raised me, but I'm not her biological son, a fact she will never let me forget. To her, I represent everything she hates about her husband, but tenfold. I'm the dark sheep of our family. Where Carson is light and kind, a promising young prosecutor, a family man, the heir to the Maddison fortune, I'm cutthroat and ambitious to a fault, a loner, begrudgingly destined to support the family business my mother would prefer to pretend does not exist.

Shane — *I'm coming home next Friday.*

Mother — *Honey, you're an adult now. You can't make these decisions last minute.*

Mother — *We've already confirmed the guest count with the caterer.*

Shane — *So add one. See you next week.*

Mother — *I see you've not settled down then?*

Mother — *It's unbecoming for a man your age to sleep around.*

Mother — *I know your father hasn't been the best example, but I'd hoped that I taught you to treat women better than that.*

I want to smash the screen against the desk. I'll never be good enough for her. A constant reminder of my father's infidelity. The spitting image of him at the age when he came crawling home to tell her he'd fathered a child in an affair.

But I'm nothing like my father. Thomas is the patriarch. A leader. I'm the family failure. When I dropped out of Yale to join the Army, I ruined my father's succession plan, and I was disowned. Cut off financially and emotionally. I think I was even written out of the will. Everything I've built, I've done without their help. But I've grown useful to my father in the last few years, as his taste for an empire has shifted in focus. Suddenly, the tolerance for my skill set is an asset. And we've rebuilt our relationship.

I can't say the same for my mother. The thought of returning home alone to be verbally picked apart makes me reconsider my decisions. Surely, staying here with Meghan couldn't be worse.

As if manifested by my thoughts, she walks past. I can

smell her before I see her, her sweet jasmine scent wrapping around me like a chokehold I can't escape. She's not special, I remind myself. She's the same as any other person. Any other person who's a pawn within the game of my job description. No one special. Not someone who deserves space in my thoughts.

Draped as she is in my blazer, I can't even make out the curve of her waist. Or those hips. I breathe a sigh of relief at the thought of a reprieve, but *fuck*, I realize as she walks down the hall, not being able to see her body does little to ease my desire. Her short stature is hidden away beneath a piece of me. It incites my body's plea to dominate her. To take that beautiful, small neck in my hand and watch her pretty mouth struggle to moan my name as she writhes beneath me.

I shake my head. I have to keep it together.

Shane — *Two then.*

Mother — *You'll bless us with the presence of a sex worker? How charming.*

Shane — *Girlfriend.*

Mother — *She's not your girlfriend if you had to pay for her, darling.*

Shane — *Can't wait for you to meet her, mother.*

Mother — *If you embarrass me, Shane, I swear to God I will make sure your father leaves you nothing in the will.*

I leave her on read to scroll through my contacts. Any woman can pretend to be my girlfriend to appease my mother. It's a few days. I only need someone to distract my family and myself. Not a love match. Shit, it doesn't even have to lead to sex. The last thing I need is a new woman to let down when she confuses orgasms with lasting feelings. I could go with an ex. I drum my fingers along the back of my phone. An ex wouldn't need filler-conversation or an explanation. My breakups have always been amicable, enough, my charm too great to hold ill will long term. I prefer it that way. For moments like this, when I need a favor.

Shane — *What are you doing next weekend?*
Erica — *Going to your brother's wedding.*
Shane — *Need a date?*
Erica — *No dummy. I'm the maid of honor.*
Erica — *Remember? That's how your brother met Abbey?*
Erica — *She's been my best friend since we were five.*
Shane — *Well, Abbey's got a date already so . . .*
Shane — *You need me.*
Erica — *You're the last thing anyone would need.*

Her words might sting if I cared. The thing is, I know she's not entirely wrong. I'm selfish and single-minded. If I found a woman who'd look past all that to fall in love with me, she'd find herself eclipsed by my life. My needs. Her individuality would be swallowed whole.

The women I know don't deserve that.

Father — *I hear you're coming home for the wedding? Don't let this derail your work.*
Shane — *Understood.*
Father — *We have three weeks. Make it happen fast.*

No one deserves the person I become for work. No, it's more than work. This is the family's business, and now it's my life. The women I know shouldn't be subjected to what I have to do for a living. Least of all, someone as promising as Meghan.

Chapter Five: Meghan

The office buzzes with potential the closer we are to the end of the day. It's been nonstop work since the merger began, and I'm not the only one working that hard. This is the final push before it's revealed who makes partner. The hunger can be seen in everyone's eyes.

Jeremy struts through the hallway, high-fiving anyone who pays him attention. His books are the biggest of the sixth years.

I roll my eyes.

I don't need to parade around the office loudly proclaiming my victories. I work hard. And that's what matters in the end. Michele wouldn't have given me point if I wasn't ready. I don't need to be flashy. I just need to keep my head down and finish strong.

I can't allow myself to be distracted.

I straighten my shoulders. I can't allow my own self-limiting beliefs to stand in the way of my success. Refocused, I exhale and resume reading through pages in hopes of finding the contracts I need. The focus lasts all of two and a half pages.

My claw clip is too tight. The twist on my hair yanks at my scalp more and more with every word. *Fuck*, I can't pay attention. My skin starts to itch with frustration, and I think I'd rather set myself on fire than continue letting meaningless words slip by. I take my hair down and allow the ends to unravel. The release of tension lets me think. The easing of frustration allows those thoughts to run coherently. I toss the clip onto the table and continue on.

It takes me a moment to register that the lack of papers turning means Shane's stopped working. I glance up to find him watching me.

"Don't look at me like that," I say. I catch him, but he doesn't look away. His eyes linger on the undone waves falling over my shoulders. There's a hunger behind it.

"What? I can't help how my face looks." He grins.

"Then keep it away from me." The last thing I need is confusing fleeting attraction for feelings.

"You want me to hide my face? Seems a little difficult, considering we have to find the lease agreement in one of these boxes before the end of the week. At this rate, we're going to spend a great deal of time together."

"Then go get me a coffee so I can work faster. The sooner we're done, the sooner we can be apart."

"Does my presence affect you that much, Meghan?"

"Nothing about you affects me, Shane. I just don't like you." I shove several boxes into the corner, separating the ones I've gone through from the ones we still have to review.

"Me?" He clutches at his chest in fake outrage.

"I'll take my coffee black, thank you." I cross my arms.

Surprisingly, Shane does as he's told. When he returns, he hands me the cup of coffee and smirks.

"Did you poison this?" I eye him with suspicion.

"What makes you think I would poison you?" His gaze flashes with something devious.

"I don't know." I sniff the coffee. It seems to smell all right. I take a tentative sip. "You seem like the type."

He laughs. "I'll take that as a compliment."

"It most certainly was not." I might have only known him for a short while, but one fact is for certain, Shane doesn't need compliments. His ego is big enough already.

Chapter Six: Shane

"So how long until you think the merger's done?" I ask. We walk back into her office. She sits behind her desk and does whatever it is that she's come in for. I don't like following her around like a puppy, but I don't have a better idea yet. I stuff my hands in my pockets.

She doesn't answer.

"A week or . . . two?" I press. My agitation overflows into an impatient tap of my foot.

"I don't know." She glances up at me briefly.

"Three or, how much longer —"

"Why do you care?" she snaps.

"Are you not good at closing quickly or?" I can't help the joy that expands in my chest as she frowns. The thinning of her lips encourages me on. I know this is for the assignment, but annoying her is becoming the bonus. "It's just a good attorney would be able to tell me how much longer." I rock back and forth on my feet, waiting for her eyebrows to pinch together and her words to lash out.

She doesn't take the bait. "Weeks longer if you keep distracting me," she mumbles into her desk.

"So you find me distracting?" I slide my thumb across my mouth to conceal my amusement.

She tilts her head, and my momentary victory is gone. This woman is five-foot-two max, at full height, chin held high. Sitting down in her chair, she barely comes up to my belt. Yet somehow, she manages to unnerve me as she glares up at me beneath her lashes.

My dick twitches. *Fuck.* Her glasses slide down her nose, but she doesn't blink, doesn't look away. Her eyes narrow at my defiance. I won't look away either, though. I don't want to miss a second of the way she stares back at me.

Then she looks away. And the moment is gone before I can seize it.

Disappointment floods through me like cold water. Every time I think I understand what she's feeling, something about her makes me second-guess myself. This is why she's just an assignment, I repeat in my head. This is nothing more than an assignment.

I walk around her office to distract myself since she won't. I start at one end and wander to the other. Four diplomas hang on the wall opposite her desk. I imagine she did that so she could admire her accomplishments all day. She seems like the type. I read the file my father had on her. Maybe not a trust fund princess, but almost. Her mother, an up-and-coming senator, is the star of her political party. Her father is a well-renowned law professor. The picture-perfect woman with her real-life perfect family.

I skim the books lining the shelf behind her desk, not to read the titles, but because it gets me closer to her without an explanation. I trail my pointer finger over each spine, The leather-bound pages holding some part of the law she must find necessary to keep close at hand. I don't take Meghan as a frivolous person. Everything in this office serves a purpose. There are no trinkets. No personal items kept for comfort. It's almost as if every part of her down to the pens she writes with were chosen . . . pieced together in a way that would add up to the outcome she wanted.

So when I see the photograph of her and some guy, I know it's not an accident either. I cross to the end of the bookshelf and hold the frame in my hands, as if touching it will tell me why the fuck this guy is so important that he gets a special spot in her curated life. I know she doesn't have a brother. So who is this guy? He's handsome, and his arm is draped over her shoulders as if he does it all the time. He's clearly very fucking interested.

"You're sure you don't have a boyfriend?" I try to keep my voice neutral, but I think I fail. I grind my teeth.

"Yes, I'm sure." She spins around in her chair, stands to snatch the picture out of my hands, and places it back on the shelf I stole it from.

"So who's that then?" I need an answer. I tell myself it's for a reason. I need to know every potential pitfall. Gather all the details before I can act. If she has a love interest, maybe I can use it against her somehow to distract her.

"That's Jeremy. We graduated law school together. He works down the hall." She sits down at her desk and pretends to go back to work. I know she's pretending because I can see the reflection of her laptop screen in her glasses. She's studying her home screen with more interest than I've seen most people watch TV.

I must really be getting on her nerves. *Good.*

"And you have a picture of him because?" My question trails off as I walk around the desk to stand beside her. I know she hates it when I get too close. I can tell it's worked when that tiny wrinkle furrows her forehead and her eyebrows push together.

"He was my secret Santa at last year's Christmas party. He got me that."

"And you keep it because?" I step closer. Everything in this office serves a purpose. So what's his?

"Why all the questions, Shane? Don't you have files to go through?" She glares at me. Or attempts to. Her head tips back as far as it can go in order to look up at me, exposing her slender neck down to the bit of collarbone peeking out beneath her shirt. I know it's meant to be dismissive. Instead, it's adorable.

I want to take her, lift her up into my arms, and kiss my way from her forehead to the buttons on her shirt. Honestly, it's blurring from want to need. I think I need to feel her excitement against me. I need to make her passionate stare transform from annoyed to watery with pleasure. And it's beginning to feel as if this need is going to be my ruin, not hers.

"Just waiting on you, boss," I say. I stuff my hands in my pockets to try and hide the bulging evidence of my thoughts.

"Are you incapable of doing due diligence without me? What are you, a first year? Am I going to have to hold your hand through this entire acquisition?"

"Sure. Or I could offer something else for you to hold if you prefer," I say.

"Obviously not your ego. I don't think anyone is strong enough for that." She bites her lip at her own cleverness.

"Ouch." I clutch my chest. "You've wounded me, Meg."

"Not as much as I'd like." She returns her attention to the papers in front of her. "And don't call me that."

"Ohhh, demanding and a sadist? It's always the quiet ones." I smirk.

"Fuck you, Shane."

"I mean, I'd rather you ask me nicely, but I guess if that's what it takes to impress the boss around here." I uncross my arms and place my hands on the desk, hovering inches over her. "It's not very professional, but that does seem to be your MO."

Her cheeks flush, and I know I've gotten under her skin.

"You're a dick, you know that?"

"Now you want to see my dick?" I lean closer. "Ms. Mayfield, how inappropriate. What will HR think of this." I know I shouldn't push her, but I can't stop. It's fun to watch the increase in frustration.

"Oh my god. Get away from me. Go far, far away." She

stands and points toward the door. "Find a contract to read. Make yourself useful."

"Afraid of a sexual harassment lawsuit? Smart woman." I tap the desk twice. "Don't worry, this can be our secret." I wink.

I start to walk out of the office, but Jeremy's sudden appearance in the doorway stops me. We eye each other. Neither of us is willing to move. The fucker straightens his shoulders and tips back his head, as if that'll make up for the height difference. His insecurity is almost as loud as his choice of tie.

"Oh, hey, Jeremy," Meghan says. Her footsteps shuffle closer until she's between us.

I wonder if she can sense the tension.

"Shane, this is Jeremy. Jeremy, this is Shane," she says, introducing us. Her voice trails off as her eyes meet mine. She gulps.

"The transfer," Jeremy says, shaking my hand. He breaks my attention from Meghan.

"Yep," I say. This fucking loser. His grip strength is childlike. I squeeze harder.

"Lateral, right?"

"Partner track," I correct.

"Ah, competition. I'm sorry you don't stand a chance."

I sense the double meaning behind his words. Before I can respond, Meghan faces him and pats his shoulder. Her touch leaves a smug grin on his face. He thinks he's won. He thinks that her being close means she's picked him instead of me.

I wish I could punch the smile from his face.

"Well, Shane and I have a room full of boxes to get through before the end of the week, so we'll see you later, okay?" She walks out of the office and motions for me to follow.

"It was nice to meet you, Jake," I say and close the door behind us.

Chapter Seven: Meghan

When I was younger, I wanted to be a princess. Not in the dress-up, play-date kind of way. I wanted to be a real princess. I consumed fairytales, romance novels, and anything I could get my hands on that fed me stories of love. I dreamt of my Prince Charming, with blond hair, blue eyes, and a kind smile that would show up one day and sweep me off of my feet to carry me into the sunset.

I had a tiara collection. Pretty makeup. Soft pink clothes with delicate silhouettes, and I hosted tea parties for my friends. I grew into the cheerleader. The rule follower. The honors student. A hopeless romantic. Never popular, but always liked. Always dating boys who were preppy, kind, and utterly unremarkable.

Growing up, I thought I was safe. I shaped myself into the mold of what society expected me to be, expecting the reward that came from becoming what they wanted me to become.

That version of myself died a long time ago. Instead of fairytales and perfect grades, I now fill myself with deadlines and client acquisition. I wake up, eat, and sleep my career. It's the one constant in my life since school. The routine that seems to hold me together.

There's been zero disruptions to my life since that one night all those years ago in May. I've made sure of it. It seemed to be working. Healing even. Until this week.

By Friday, I find myself both dreading and dreaming of work. I don't know whether to cry or celebrate the thought of an entire weekend without Shane. There's something about being around that man that makes my head spin. It's like when I'm near him, it pulls out a different version of myself, one that I didn't even know existed.

Stupid. I shake my head. That doesn't make any sense. I've known him a total of four days, five if I count today. Really, less than forty hours. Not enough time to make an impact on a sane person—but I'm not sane, I think.

The schedule is light today, which should mean less one-on-one time than we've had so far, creating a much-needed opportunity to regain clarity on the whole thing. I squint my eyes, and from a distance, he's not as handsome. I chance some glances every now and then, not enough to draw his attention, but enough to put him on trial for my emotions.

His face is cleanly shaven, showcasing his sharp features—his cheekbones and strong jawline. I can't decide what it is exactly about him that draws me in. Maybe it's those lips, so full and soft, a warm contradiction to the near-permanent scowl on his face. Maybe it's his hair. The dark ends falling into his deep brown eyes when he leans too far forward. That might be my favorite, I think. I like to watch him run his hands through it, those long fingers pushing it away. Or maybe his nose, strong and defined. Everything about him coming together to create something brutally beautiful.

Or it could be his thick, expressive eyebrows that narrow in suspicion as he catches me looking. *Shit.*

I focus back on my desk, hoping to find work undone to swallow me whole, and instead, I hear the muffled sound of footsteps.

"Did you need something, Meghan?" Shane asks as he walks into my office.

I really should start locking my door.

I have to swivel in my chair if I want to see him as I speak. I don't. It's hard enough to resist the urge to hide my face in my hands. "Hmm, no, just trying to get my work done." I stare pointedly at my emails, avoiding eye contact, begging the universe to send me something important.

Nothing comes.

Clara and I really need a better system here. Maybe a hand signal to put an important call through when I need to escape. I glance over at her desk, beyond the glass wall of my office, hoping to catch her attention, but she's not even there.

"Oh yeah? Because it seemed like you might be distracted. But maybe there's a lot on your mind? Care to tell me what it is? I'm sure I could help you think through it." He eases himself against my desk. Resting there. So close I can feel the warmth of his body.

I gulp. My thoughts turn erotic. I can't help it. I'm so close, I think I start to want him. It's been too long since I wanted someone. I stare. I study, desperately hoping to find evidence or an outline of a bulge. Hoping to see the physical proof that I affect him as much as he affects me. And god, I want to know what it looks like. If I could just feel it. Run my hands up his thighs and gently caress my fingertips over him.

It would be too much to hope for him to return these urges. I risk another look. He's watching me with such a pained expression that I feel that familiar embarrassment creep back in. This is a workplace. I can't have these thoughts. Shouldn't have them. Even if he feels the same, by some miracle, we wouldn't make it past a one-night stand. He's a man, not a character in a novel. The fantasies I have are just that, and dreams are no more than fiction.

My unease is lessened by the appearance of my friends. If Kennedy and Michael notice the tension, they don't show it. They launch right into conversations about dinner and drinks and the Friday night plans they've made for us all, kindly overlooking the way Shane sits perched on top of my desk.

"You're coming, right?" Kennedy turns to Shane. "To get drinks, at least. It's tradition."

"Tradition is a strong word." I relax a little. No one's said anything. Not even a raised eyebrow. Maybe I'm hiding it better than I thought. "Occasional outing, perhaps." I don't usually go. I didn't last week, even though Kennedy started the office's Friday night out, and she's the closest thing I have to a best friend. We all continue to show up because of our work schedules rather than some deep bond that unites our habits. It seems the longer we work for this firm, the fewer friends we have outside of it.

"Don't be like that," Michael cuts in. "We're nearing the end of all this." He waves his hands to the boxes stacked around the room. "Just because you gave up one of our traditions doesn't mean the rest of us did."

"Too soon." Kennedy slaps his arm.

I feel Shane's focus flicker to me, but I avoid him. I can always feel him watching me. The weight of his attention lays heavy on my skin and heats my cheeks. He's probably afraid I'll swoon at his smallest gesture. Maybe Kennedy can't tell yet, but I know I've made my feelings obvious to him. But I won't swoon. I'm not going to break my professionalism in front of the others. This time, I mean it. He's not worth it. I won't embarrass myself by putting my desire on display for the entire office. I can imagine their judgment now. What a shame. She was going to make partner and threw it all away for a guy. She's so unethical. She's a whore.

"So this . . . tradition. What time does it start?" Shane asks eventually. His gaze still lingers on me, but I refuse to turn my head.

"We usually meet about eight or nine. Assuming we make it out of here alive. There's drinks, dancing, karaoke if Meredith over there gets drunk enough." Kennedy points to the office across the hall. "It's a good time. You should come."

"Sounds fun. Text me the address," Shane says.

"Sure, oh shit." Kennedy looks at her watch. "We're late

for that one meeting. Come on, Michael. Meghan can text you the details." She waves a hand in my general direction.

"What meeting?" Michael asks as Kennedy drags him away.

"Shut up," she whispers.

I watch as they hurry off down the hall and into another conference room. I don't know if she planned this or if it was an accident, but I'm left alone with a grinning Shane and a lot of anxiety.

"Yeah, Meghan. Text me the details," he says softly.

"I don't have your number." I realize I'm still eye-level with his dick. I need to get laid so I can focus and stop fixating on him. That's all it is. I'm just lonely. Anyone will do.

"I can fix that. Give me your phone." He holds out his hand.

"Fine." I sigh. I reach into my back pocket, unlock the screen, and hand it over. While he's distracted, I push myself back a little bit to create space between my face and his body. He's just a man, I repeat to myself. He's not special. He's just a man. A very tall, handsome man with sharp cheekbones, deep brown eyes, and a voice that makes me want to melt into the ground. But that doesn't make him matter. I can find someone else to take up the space of my attention.

"Text me the details. I can't wait." He grins as if he can read my thoughts.

Chapter Eight: Shane

I gave her my number in hopes that she'd make the first move. I wanted her to feel safe. To give her the freedom to approach me outside of work on her own terms. I told myself that if she wanted me, then I could allow myself to give in to my desires. That it wouldn't be wrong if I gave her what she wanted. As if her interest and her consent were one and the same. I thought I could see it written on her pretty little face. The way her throat bobbed anytime I stood too close. The way she'd pick at her nails if I made eye contact too long. I'm good at reading people. But maybe sweet, soft Meghan can read me, too. And that passion I see just under the surface is reserved for someone else, someone normal.

It was delusional to imagine a scenario in which my actions would lead to her beneath me. If she won't give in to me now, she definitely won't when this is all over.

I lie on my bed and stare up at the coffered ceiling, unable to bring myself to do anything besides replay this last week in my head. I should've kept my original plan—stay away from her, make anyone else the target. I rack my brain to try and figure out where I went wrong. I thought she wanted me—that's what derailed my plan. The little side glances. The way she'd bite her lip every time she was caught looking up at me. I swear I could feel her pulse when I got too close. Sense her excitement. And I let my dick start to make the decisions.

Fuck. I rub the palms of my hands over my eyes. Even now, I can't stop myself. Understanding does little to ease the tension around what I want. I tap my fingers against my phone as if it might light up with her number. But it doesn't. I can't even close my eyes because I'm too afraid to see her face in my imagination. Those eyes. Those lips. If I can't stop picturing her in our time apart, I'll go crazy.

And then I don't know what I'll do.

Maybe I can convince her the Prince Charming she's so clearly dreaming of isn't the best option. Maybe she'll never admit to wanting what I have to offer, but maybe I can persuade her not to say no.

And that's why I can't get any closer. She's a name on a to-do list. She'd never want to be more. How could she? How would I begin to explain to Meghan that I want to dominate her?

Should I save that for our first date? After I ruin the biggest deal of her career. Tell her over dessert that the thought of her tears makes me hard. That I dream of hearing her beg and plead as I force one more orgasm from her body.

My phone vibrates, and I nearly choke in relief. If it's not her, I'll fucking lose it. I need to get this woman out of my system before I do something I regret.

Unknown—*589 May Rd. Eight o'clock.*

Shane—*I thought you ghosted me.*

Meghan—*I def considered it*

Shane—*What made you change your mind?*

Meghan—*Well it wasn't your personality*

Shane—*My looks then? Makes sense.*

Meghan—*You're so full of yourself*

Shane—*You would be too if you looked like me*

Meghan—*On second thought, don't come tonight*

Shane—*Why? You want me to come over instead . . . awfully forward of you. Send the address.*

Meghan—*you wish*

Shane—*I don't have to.*

Chapter Nine: Meghan

It takes me longer than I'd like to admit to pick an outfit, and somehow, I choose the same pair of jeans and t-shirt I always wear. To say I'm nervous is an understatement. My palms sweat as I turn left down the street toward the bar, Lenny's. I go almost weekly, even though I don't like it, and I'm sober. The drinking isn't what bothers me now. I'm past that. It's the people. Social interactions make me so nervous my heart races, or I guess one particular interaction does.

I don't bother to look at my reflection in the windows before I walk inside because I don't want to second-guess myself. I'm confident, I practice my affirmations, and I have nothing to prove.

The bar lights are dim, and the music is loud as I walk over to where I see Kennedy and Sophia seated. They look stunning in their silky blouses with their perfect hair. Clearly having left the office minutes before, they still manage to look happy and carefree, laughing over their martinis. That's the life I thought I would have. Manicured. Social yet sophisticated. Drinking top-shelf liquor with my friends in warmly lit legacy bars, wearing my designer shoes, and paying with my metal credit card.

I fucked that up last year. I used alcohol to drink away my thoughts and found I couldn't make it through my day without a little liquid courage. My parents were able to get me into rehab quietly. Not for my well-being. They couldn't afford the scandal of a daughter who violated the code of ethics. Certainly not in an election year.

"Oh, I love your shirt," Sophia croons as I sit down. She offers me a half smile then her attention goes back to her phone. Sophia only uses our presence to bide her time until she finds the best-looking person in the bar. It's still too early for someone notable, so her friendship will be sporadic as she searches tonight's playing field.

I don't really like Sophia, and I definitely don't believe her. I thank her anyway. Adding, "I didn't realize you were coming straight from the office." I pick at a loose thread on the hem of my arm. Of course Sophia would look better than everyone else. That's one of the many reasons she always goes home with the best-looking person. I might not like her, but I do admire her fearlessness to go after what she wants.

"We overworked," Sophia says, laughing. "But it had to be done." Sophia's going to make partner. I can almost guarantee it. Her billable hours are higher than anyone's, even Jeremy's. That means there's one more spot left.

"To the partner path." Kennedy holds up her glass.

"The partner path," we say in unison, clinking our glasses together. I spill a bit of my water on my shirt as I take a sip.

"Besides, you look so comfortable and relaxed, Meg." Sophia smiles at me as she pats my hand. "I'm super jealous."

I dab a napkin at my shirt. Our interactions are always fake, much like the rest of our night. We talk about mundane things. Mostly we try to avoid talking about work and end up talking about it anyway. We don't have much in common besides that. But it's never just a harmless conversation. It's always a contest. Always sizing each other up. Ready to make the others feel inferior or file away a bit of information that could be used against them later. It's probably why I drank so much, I think as I sip my water. I'm not really sure this is so fun anymore now that I can think coherently.

This was a stupid idea. This isn't how I want to spend my night. I just want to go home. I check my watch. It's still too early to leave and be normal. I want to say I'm tired, but I used that excuse last time. I consider feigning a headache. I haven't used that one before. I suppose I could wait until the appetizers to decide for sure. I did promise Kennedy I'd at least try.

The moment the food arrives at the table, I shove a ranch-covered mozzarella stick into my mouth for something to do. Shane walks in a bite later, and I nearly choke. His stupid text messages run through my head like closed captioning I can't turn off. *He doesn't wish.* What does that even mean? Does he want me then? Does he think he can just have me? The thought makes my face flush in hope then anger. He can't just have me. I'm not an object. Is my crush on him so obvious that he thinks he can just toy with me until he's ready? God, what's wrong with me? I'm probably just another option he'll keep in his rotation. He's clearly a playboy. A womanizer. Someone who would only enjoy hurting me and breaking my heart.

He sits down, choosing to not take the open seat next to me, keeping two people between us the rest of the night. I try to rationalize the change in behavior. Just because we work together on the same case doesn't make us friends. He has no reason to sit next to me. But I do think he was flirting. Maybe he's being coy. I can't possibly be making up this tension between us. It's not one-sided. I reread his text messages beneath the table to convince myself. He wants me. I know he does. But just like the rest of the week, any hint of his desire for me evaporates before I have the chance to latch on.

"What'cha doing?" Jeremy says into my ear.

I jerk back at his unexpected appearance and lean away. His hot breath smells like whiskey and makes my skin want to turn itself inside out.

"Miss me?" He places his arm around my shoulders and pulls me against him, nearly suffocating me with the equally repulsive smell of his aftershave. His skin feels clammy against mine. I'm desperate to get away, but he drags me closer. From beneath the crook of his arm, I think I see a flash of anger cross Shane's face. His hands clench into fists on the table before he relaxes and hides himself. I can't see him as well as I'd like through the people beside us. Their bodies are blocking my line of sight. Their laughter is making the space between us feel too vast to cross.

Jeremy seems determined not to let me go. I should've made a move on Shane when he got here. If there was ever a time to find out what he's feeling, it would be tonight. I could still change seats to sit beside him. Find an excuse to stay. Let my thigh brush against his. Touch his arm when he says something funny.

Sophia beats me to my own plan, her manicured hand clutching his bicep, her blonde head thrown back in laughter that doesn't meet her face. She does it better than I could. Shane seems to agree. He offers her a smile. She makes him laugh. He smiles even brighter and leans forward, their heads so close together I'm surprised his lips don't brush her forehead.

Shane would be interested in Sophia. He's a single man. He's probably interested in everyone. The smiles, the teasing, and tension between us, it's not special. I'm not special. He's a flirt. He's an attractive, flirtatious man who's just existing while I'm the one magnifying every move he makes in hopes of proving his affection.

"Did you hear me, babe?" Jeremy asks. He squeezes my shoulder.

I hate when men call me babe. I try to shrug him off.

"Anyways, I was saying," he continues on, finally dropping his heavy arm from around the back of my neck. "That deal I closed last week put my billable hours near the top."

Jeremy does his best to draw me into a conversation around how impressive he is, and I force myself to pay attention in order to avoid meeting Shane's eyes. The bar is loud, but we're still close. I lean in despite my desire to run and hide. I try to listen to his words but find my mind wandering regardless. Then I try to watch his mouth, as if seeing it move will help solidify the words into meaning. When that doesn't work, I change the subject. Hoping if we talk about me, I'll at least be able to feign engagement.

As I start to recount the story of my week, Sophia, then Shane, disappears around the corner. My stomach churns with disappointment that feels like acid. I can't remember what I was saying or why I'm even here. I want the table to swallow me whole and disappear into a new day, a fresh start. Unfortunately, without alcohol, there's no way to escape my emotions but to feel through them. And I don't want to process that here in front of everyone else. I need to go home, preferably not alone.

So when Jeremy puts his hand on my leg, I don't move away, even when the familiar panic tastes like bile in my throat. I don't move when his alcohol-laced breath whispers in my ear. And when his words ask to take me home, I actually consider it. It's not the first time Jeremy has tried to sleep with me. But tonight is the first night I consider letting him.

Chapter Ten: Shane

I don't know what she's getting at. I didn't take her for the kind of person who plays games, but it seems as if I misjudged. I watch her snuggle into Jermey. I don't know which pisses me off more, being wrong or being disappointed. That sweet face presents innocence only to mask the siren beneath. I should've known better. Father was right. And that makes it all so much worse. She's not a woman unlucky to cross my path, destined for more. She's my assignment. And she's probably whispering in his ear about her plans to take him home. To fuck him, just to spite me.

I shake my head. How did this happen? I left the table for a minute, and now she's cuddling up with that douchebag.

I can't afford to be distracted. I run my hands through my hair.

But the thoughts don't stop. It'll be the luckiest damn night of his life. A beautiful woman like that on her knees. Or splayed out naked on her back, her thighs spread and hungry to be fucked. My hands tighten around my glass. He doesn't deserve her. He wouldn't even know what to do with her. I'm not jealous, I tell myself. I'm pragmatic. Her romantic life complicates what needs to happen next. The fucker will notice when she's gone. And judging by the way he watched her and then watched me, he'll definitely remember if I was the last one to be seen with her.

I consider my options. I could go after them if they leave. It would make a scene, but it'd prevent her from making a disappointing decision. She would thank me later. He looks like he doesn't know how to fuck. He'd basically use her body to masturbate. A complete waste. She's a goddess. She should be worshiped, her orgasms drawn out and savored.

Sophia keeps talking to me, but I can no longer hear her. Occasionally, I lean over and smile, keeping her placated. She could be a good alibi. I see her drink empty and wave down the bartender and order her another to distract her from me. She smiles up at me so brightly from beneath her lashes I think it's worked. Her blue eyes are glazed over. It won't be much longer until she's too drunk to remember me or where I'm at.

"You have to keep up," she says as she takes the drink. Her words slur together, and she places her hand on my arm to steady herself. A little bit of the drink spills on me, but I school my face not to react. I hate stains on my clothing, but she could be useful, and I don't want to scare her away.

"You're better at this than me," I say. I swirl my drink. The ice has started to melt.

"What else am I better at than you," she says. She leans over to be closer.

"Wouldn't you like to know?"

Chapter Eleven: Meghan

I'm tired of watching Shane and Sophia. I'm tired of the loud music and dim lights. My head hurts from wearing my contacts too long, and my stomach growls in a desperate plea for real food. I think I'm getting too old for this. I watch everyone around me having fun, laughing, drinking. My heart starts to race as if I'm having a panic attack. The drinking.

I play with the straw in my water. It's been months since I had my last drink. At first, I thought I'd never be able to go out to the bars again with my friends. That thought was devastating. Would they think I was no longer fun? Would they want to be around me? But none of those worst-case scenarios came true. I was relieved. I got to keep my life and my friends. Now I think something far worse has happened. Sober me learned a truth I tried really hard my whole life to avoid. *I was never happy.* This was never supposed to be my life. And the drinking was the only thing that made any of it bearable.

"I'll be right back," I say. I set down my water and head to the bathroom. I don't look back to see if Jeremy heard me. He tried to follow me to the bar the last time I stood up, and I need to put some distance between us that he can't cross. I thought maybe I could give this a shot. Sleep with him, that is. It's been a while since I got laid. There are worse options than Jeremy Adams. He's handsome, in a frat boy kind of way. But then he kept offering to buy me drinks all night and trying to replace my water, then hinting at the blow he brought with him, as if that would make me more likely to enjoy being with him.

I can hide in the bathroom a little bit, buy myself some time, and find an excuse to leave. If nothing else, read through my unread emails until Kennedy, Meredith, or even Caroline can come save me.

I'm so confident in my plan that initially, I don't hear Jeremy behind me. The warning starts with the sound of his footsteps moving too close too quickly. Then the smell of alcohol as his hot breath moves wordlessly against my ear. My mind races with solutions that don't involve screaming or drawing unnecessary attention to us. I don't want to overreact, but the fear turns into terror as his hand grips my shoulder.

"You weren't going to invite me to the party?" he slurs.

I try to shrug him off. "I'm just going to the bathroom," I say.

"Come on, don't be like that." He gets closer, and I step away. It's the wrong move. It's allowed him to back me against the wall. "I just want to kiss you," he says.

"Jeremy, no." I push against his chest. I need to get around him.

He stumbles backward. His movements are delayed, so I know he's too drunk to be reasoned with. I need to get back to the table.

"Come on, don't be so boring."

"Jeremy, no. I don't want to—"

My sentence is cut off as Shane grabs him by the neck.

I barely have time to blink before Shane punches Jeremy in the face, and he's splayed out on the floor. But Shane doesn't stop there. He kicks Jeremy until his face is bloodied and he's curled in the fetal position, crying, pleading for him to stop.

I look around. Surely there's someone who can stop this. But we're tucked out of view down a long, quiet hallway, far away from the loud sounds of the other patrons and no one seems to be coming to help.

"Shane, stop!" I yell. I hesitate to pull him off of Jeremy for fear he'll hit me too in the struggle, but when he kicks him once, twice more, I decide there's no other option.

"Shane, no. He's not worth it." I grab Shane's arm and pull him to me. I tense, ready for his anger to spill over toward me, but he stills, breathing in deeply, as if my voice snaps him from his rage.

He's quiet, aside from catching his breath. He stays still. Judging by the way he watches me, I think he can sense my fear. It's as if he's searching my face for some sign of what to do next. I'm repulsed. His usually soft brown eyes look black. His cheekbones appear sharper in the dim lighting, transforming his face from beautifully handsome to cold and ruthless. Even more so when I glance down and see his knuckles covered in Jeremy's blood.

"Where do you think you're going?" Shane asks as I step away.

"Far away from you," I say.

He pulls me to him so hard and so suddenly that I stumble into his chest. Despite the fear I felt when Jeremy got near, Shane's body seems to have the opposite effect. His chest feels nice against my head. His hands on my arms spark much-needed warmth along my skin. And as Jeremy stirs on the floor, it feels good to know I'm not alone. But I don't let myself get complacent.

"Get off of me," I say.

"No," he says.

"Get. Off. Me." I try to take another step, but his fingers grip my arm harder.

"No," he grits out.

I can tell I've annoyed him by the way he clenches and releases his jaw. The thin veil of safety evaporates just as quickly as it settles over me.

"No?" I pull away with great effort. *Fuck him.* I didn't ask him to get involved. He did it himself. If I'm such an inconvenience to him, he can go.

"No. Not until I know you're safe." He tugs on my hand, but this time, he walks purposely toward our table before I can wiggle free.

I follow behind, not for lack of trying. His fingers only dig into mine harder as he pulls me faster. His steps are so large I have to jog to keep up.

"Meghan doesn't feel good, so I'm going to see her home," he says to no one in particular. He puts his jacket around my shoulders and holds my purse. "Goodnight." He doesn't give me time to say anything.

I stumble behind him. My hand is still in his, my other trying to straighten the jacket so it doesn't fall from my shoulders.

"Where are you taking me?" I ask. I'm concerned I've traded one villain for another. My judgment seems questionable. More often than not, I'm drawn in by the worst types of men.

"Home. Are you not listening?" he snaps.

"I can see myself home, thank you." I yank my hand free and nearly fall over from the force.

The air is cold outside the bar, and I slip my arms into Shane's jacket. His cologne twists its way around my senses and wraps me in his essence. He smells so good. I long to take a deep breath to savor the woody spice but would rather suffocate than fill myself with him. I don't want to be here. I never wanted to put myself in another position to be saved, for my safety to rest in the hands of another. It pisses me off. That, and the exhaustion that replaces the adrenaline in my veins makes me trip as I hurry across the sidewalk to hail a taxi.

"Did he get you drunk?" Shane's hands reach out to steady my shoulders.

"What? No." I jerk my shoulder away from him. I don't

want him touching me anymore. I can't fucking think when he's touching me.

"Then why were you acting like a slut all night? Did you want to fuck him, or were you just trying to make me jealous?"

"Fuck you, Shane." It's like a slap in the face. The words sting so badly that tears form in my eyes, and I have to look away to avoid the onslaught of emotion bubbling inside. *Slut.* I repeat the words in my head. It's so familiar. Men have said it to me before. It's not wrong if I'm a slut. It's not assault if I dressed like I wanted it. There's no power in my own sexuality. Only power if a man finds me sexual.

The tears fall faster. That's what I get for thinking he might be different. But I should've known better.

All men are the same.

Chapter Twelve: Shane

I regret the words immediately. I wanted to be harsh, to convey that I'm not some Prince Charming trying to save her, but I've overstepped. Her perfect little face deflates before my eyes. Her soft lips pull down, her eyebrows scrunch together in what looks an awful lot like hurt. She turns away from me before I can say more.

That's right, I'm not a good guy, don't fall for me. I can't bring myself to actually say the words, however. I want to fix it. But I know doing so will only cause more harm in the long run. I do the only thing I know to do. I grab her and drag her back to me.

"Where are we going?" she asks as she struggles against me.

It makes my dick go hard. See, I remind myself, not a good guy.

"I'm taking you home." I clench my teeth. I have to stay focused. "Shut up and get in the car."

"No," she yells. I swear she even stomps her foot.

"It wasn't a question." I push her toward the door. She won't escape me. I don't care if she hates me. At least I'll know she's safe and far as fuck away from that pathetic excuse for a man.

I see the challenge rise up in her eyes. She looks around to find the best path to make her run, but my patience is thinning. I won't let her get away from me again. I cross my arms against my chest. I'm bigger than she is. I'll block any path she tries to take.

"I'm not going anywhere with you," she says.

"I'm not leaving you alone with them." It's a fact. No one in there cares about her as much as I do, clearly. They were all perfectly content to allow Jeremy to follow her into a dark hallway.

"I don't need you to protect me."

I laugh. She has no idea how right she is. "I'm not trying to protect you. Either you get in this car, or I'll go back in there and finish what I started." It's the most honest statement I can offer her at this moment. Because I will if she leaves me right now. I'll go back there and kick the final breath out of his lungs.

She considers me for a moment, and I realize I've found her weakness. She's too good. Too virtuous. Even more of a reason for her to get far, far away from me. If I were a moral man, the white knight she probably yearns for, I'd scare her off, drive her away. But I'm a bad man. And she seems to bring out the worst in me. That part is desperate to find a way to make this work. To find a way to keep her and finish the assignment.

"Fine. But I'm not going to fuck you just because you think I'm a whore, and you're the good man saving me."

"Oh, I know." I smile bigger. "I wasn't asking."

Chapter Thirteen: Meghan

I promised myself I'd never be in the position to be hurt again. For years, I've avoided men. I made sure to never be alone with them. Dated only those I'd known long enough to verify there was no history of domestic or sexual abuse.

Until Shane.

All those years of honing my self-preservation instincts failed me the second Shane bumped against me in the office. For whatever reason, my body doesn't register him as a threat. It draws me closer. And it's led me to be in a position I've feared since the day of my assault. I'm alone with a man, with no agency, and without anyone knowing where I'm at. The worst part is, a piece of me wishes he'd done all this to make a move.

"Don't make a scene," Shane says as we get out of the car in front of my apartment building. The streets are empty this time of night. There are no witnesses.

Before I can blink, he's rounded the car to help me out of my door. I don't take the hand he holds out in offering. "I'm more than capable of seeing myself inside," I say. The words come out with less malice than I intend as I stand and stumble over the curb, and he captures my body with his arms.

"Get off me." I push him away and try to walk toward the entryway. I don't know how he knew I lived here. I certainly didn't tell him. "You're not coming in with me," I say, louder, because obviously he's not smart enough to understand un-spoken boundaries. I muster all the hatred I can. I don't know why he's following me, anyway. He called me a slut. He went out of his way to say he's not asking to fuck me. Of course he's not. He doesn't want to. He's really made that point crystal clear, and somehow, I'm so fucked up that I still wish he did. Tears burn my eyes as I try to think of anything else.

Shane doesn't respond. He catches up to me in three lazy steps and intertwines his hand in mine as he smiles at the doorman who's finally appeared. He strides confidently across the marble foray to the elevators as if this is our normal Friday night, and we do this all the time.

"Keep your mouth shut. I know that's hard for you," he whispers just so I can hear. The possessive grip between my fingers squeezes as the elevator doors open, and another couple steps out. He smiles at them. Like he's normal. Like this is all normal.

"Fuck you." I glare at him, but our height difference makes my normally stern assertion feel more like a temper tantrum. I yank my fingers out of his hold.

"Get in," he says, amused. His soft chuckle at my reaction doesn't exactly help that feeling either.

"What if I scream?" I ask as the doors close, suddenly acutely aware that there's no longer an escape. I'm trapped, alone with Shane. The walls seem to tighten around us as the lift swoops upward with a smooth metallic whir.

"You wouldn't."

"What if I do?" I want him to say something comforting. Or to apologize. I stare up at his deep brown eyes, hoping to find a sign that I'm safe. But there's no safety written on his angular features, which become sharper and more brutal as the ride goes on. Out of my peripheral, I can see the floor lights blink higher and higher as we pass each level, counting down to the unknown. Shane might be bigger, but I'm not exactly demure enough to kidnap. I'm short, but I'm pretty strong. I can put up a fight. I won't go quietly.

He sighs. "Then I won't know you're safe. And then I'll

have no choice but to go back to that bar and make sure Jeremy *can never look* at you again, let alone touch you. Which is what *I would've done* had you not stopped me in the first place."

I think of Jeremy's *bloody face* and shiver. A part of me says he's bluffing. This man is a lawyer who got in a lucky punch. Jeremy was knocked out before any actual fighting could start. Surely Shane wouldn't seek out violence. He wouldn't beat a man to the point of real harm. But the other, louder part of me isn't so sure.

"How do you know where I live?" It takes a second for the words to come out. Maybe he's a violent man. He could've killed Jeremy. Would have, according to him, had I not stepped in.

Maybe I can leave him in the elevator. Escape to a different floor, wait a little until I'm sure he's gone, and take the stairs. Or I could pretend to live somewhere else. I can wait him out. He'll lose interest eventually.

The elevator chimes as we reach my floor, and his hand is quick to find the small of my back.

"Come on," he says as he nudges me forward.

"Give me my purse." I stumble slightly over my words. I'm careful to take small steps. I sling the strap around my shoulder. I need a plan. I unzip the bag. I need to buy some time. He's not going to let me go. He knows where I live. I find my keys at the bottom of the purse and hold my keys between my fingers like my mother taught me. I formulate my plan with every step. My apartment is the second to last down the hall. I have a few seconds to make a decision. I can sprint away, hoping to make it to the elevators before he can. Or I can fight. I don't know if I'm strong enough to overpower him, but I definitely know I'm not fast enough. I take a deep breath. I fist my keys tighter. We're five doors away now. I think my answer is fight.

"Oh, Meghan." Shane shoves my back into the wall. "I thought you were smarter than that." It's the surprise that takes the air from my lungs. He presses his body into mine as he traps my wrists and disarms me of my keys.

"Let me go." I struggle to get away. Stupid man and his stupid strength.

"As much as I love your attempt, I can't until I get you home." He smiles as he steps back, my keys now in his hand furthest from me, the other tying me to him once more.

"Stop, Shane. I can walk on my own, and I can open my own damn door." I reach across him for my keys, but he's too quick. He dangles them above my head, far outside of my reach.

"You're shaking. Barely able to walk. And now you want me to leave you here and hope for the best? Look how well that worked out for you at the bar."

"Fuck you. I can look after myself. I said I'm not drunk."

"Oh, I know. Soda water with a lime in a tall glass. I watched you all night. That's why you don't like to go out sometimes, isn't it? You've been sober six months. Is that why you tried to get away from him? Or did you really want to take him into the bathroom? Are you that desperate to get laid you'd settle for that?"

He watched me all night. I can't stop the warmth that spreads over my body. "Is that why you punched him?"

"I punched him because he touched you." He glares down at me.

No, I can't like that. I can't find comfort in the thought of violence. I shouldn't feel safer knowing he's hurt anyone that touched me. Anger and loyalty are not one and the same. Anger doesn't mean he has feelings for me. Anger doesn't make me safe.

"Stop it, Shane. Just stop." I try to push away the thought that he cares. Because of all the thoughts I've had tonight, that one is too dark to entertain.

"Stop what?"

"Stop pretending like you care when you don't."

He snorts, seemingly offended. "I wouldn't waste my time."

I'm not worth his time, I repeat to myself as he unlocks my door, forcing me inside my own home. He wouldn't waste his time on me. I don't understand how he can be so concerned and disinterested at the same time.

"Get away from me. I'm sure Sophia is expecting you," I snap. Saying it out loud is like a weight off of my heart. I hadn't realized how deeply that had been bothering me all night. I drop my purse on the floor. I don't bother to set it on the sideboard in my foyer. There's no reason for manners or pleasantries. I want to escape his presence as quickly as possible, and preferably, behind a locked door. I move to slip off his jacket, but Shane is in my personal space before I can manage.

"Aww, are you jealous, Meg?" He places a hand on my face.

"Don't call me that." I slap his hand away.

"Hmm, what should I call you then?" He steps closer.

"Meghan. My name is Meghan. Unless you've forgotten. Because I'm sure we're all the same to you."

"So it is jealousy." He grins.

I hate how handsome he is when he smiles. Not the leers he so often sends in my direction. This is his real smile. The one that lights up his eyes in a way that steals my breath and threatens my heart. It's not a comforting gesture. It's more devious. Like there's something sadistic right behind those raised eyebrows and lopsided grin that makes me want to dive into bed and let him have his way.

Instead, I confront him. "I saw you," I say. I don't want to change the subject. I don't want him avoiding what he's done.

"You did, did you? Tell me, what is it you think you saw?"

"I saw you get her an *Uber*."

"And that means what to you?"

"It means nothing to me. I'm just stating what happened."

"I called a drunk girl an *Uber* to get home safely. I hardly think that warrants your anger. Not yet at least." There's that spark again behind his expression.

I cross my arms against my chest and refuse to meet his eyes. I could just walk away and leave this conversation behind me. Surely he wouldn't follow me past the living room uninvited.

"Come on, tell me, what do you think happened," he presses.

"You fucked her."

"I fucked her?" He laughs like it's the most outrageous thing he's ever heard. "In the bar? Tell me, how long was I gone? All of four minutes? Is that how long you think I last, Meghan? Is that what you're used to." He brushes his knuckles across my cheek.

"I don't want to talk about this." My face is hot beneath his gentle touch. I don't know why I brought it up. It's bad enough I feel this way, and I don't need him to ridicule me on top of everything else. I shouldn't have said that much. I step around him.

"Oh no, no, no. You don't get to bring this up and then shut down the conversation. If you're going to be mad at me, at least let me deserve it first."

"I'm not mad. I don't care. You can fuck whoever you like. Just leave me alone."

He traps me against the wall so I can't walk away.

"Is that so?" He puts his hands on either side of my head, his body leaning toward mine. No part of him touches me, but it sends my pulse racing regardless. My body feels as if it's on fire. Every piece of me is alert, hoping for the slightest bit of contact.

"Yes." This time, I don't cower. I meet his gaze and hold it, even though it hurts my neck to look up at him from the angle he's trapped me in. I refuse to show he's affecting me. Even if it consumes me in the process.

He smirks. Those stupid lips twist into a smug grin that makes me want to stand on my tiptoes and wipe away his victory.

"So I could go right now to her apartment and you wouldn't care?"

"Nope."

"I think you're lying." He leans down. His breath caresses my skin.

"And I think you're repulsive," I say, leaning closer.

He doesn't respond for a second. And then sighs, pushing off the wall slightly to allow me to slip away. Only when I'm a good distance apart can I breathe again. But for some reason, relief feels a lot like disappointment.

"I didn't fuck her, Meghan." He runs his hands through his hair. "Shit. I got her a car because she was drunk. I didn't go home with her. I made sure she was safe. That was all. Then I came right back inside to find Jeremy stalking you like a pred-ator." He shoves his hands in his pockets and turns to face me fully. "I was mad that you let him get that close to you, and I called you a name I didn't mean. I'm not saying it was right. I just wanted you to know why I did it."

I watch his eyes to find the deception but come up with nothing. Although I do notice that wasn't an apology either.

"You didn't get her drunk to sleep with her?" I ask. If I'm going to make myself vulnerable, I might as well know eve-rything.

He laughs deeply, genuinely, and steps toward me again. His hand is back to my face. He strokes my cheek softly. He moves closer. It seems he's always trying to stand as close to me as he can. I can't tell if it's a power move to remind me how small I am in comparison, both physically and metaphorically. Or if he wants to touch me the way I long to touch him.

"That's what you're concerned about? I wouldn't sleep with Sophia. And definitely not when she's drunk."

My body relaxes as his words replay. It's like an exhale creeps down my skin and cools my limbs. But if I overthink too long, that calm begins to fade. Should I be excited? Does that mean I like him? Does his reassurance mean he likes me?

"I'd say it's because I'm a gentleman, but that would be a lie." His touch is no longer tender. His fingers grip my jaw as he tips back my face. It's like he's searching me. Whatever he finds makes his decision. He leans closer and softly kisses my forehead.

"W-what?"

His fingers grip me harder as he laughs darkly at my surprise. "But that's a story for another time." He kisses me once more.

I hate myself as I lean into it.

"Do me a favor, Meghan, okay? Don't leave your apartment tonight. I'd like to keep you safe while I still can."

Chapter Fourteen: Shane

I wait until I hear the door lock to her apartment before leaving. Even then, it takes me a few minutes to walk down the hall to the elevator. I tell myself it's out of an abundance of caution. I need to make sure no one's followed her. I'm not overreacting. It's about her safety.

I replay our interactions in my mind. I don't typically feel guilty. But when I think back to finding her with Jeremy, I do regret what I said. I was mad. Mad at the thought that she might actually want him. Mad at her for being so careless that she'd let herself be alone with a man like that. Then again, she let herself be alone with me. I'm not much better, just a different kind of monster.

Perhaps she has a kink for danger. There was shock in her eyes when I said I wasn't a gentleman, but there was also delight. I think it excited her almost as much as it excites me. I want to go back there and feel her pulse jump as I hold her down by her neck and thrust inside. I bet if I tried, I'd find the door unlocked. Her waiting for me. On her bed. Or getting into the shower. She might not admit it just yet, but I know deep down inside she's begging for it, and I'll find proof in just how wet I make her.

I half expect a text asking me to come back. Surely she's just as close to giving in to impulse as I am. But the text never comes. And I convince myself to step into the elevator, feeling something like hope.

That fragile feeling disappears by the next morning. The

only text message I have when I wake up is from my father, demanding a meeting. I don't consider avoiding him. I brush my teeth, throw on sweatpants and a sweatshirt, and head out the door. My driver, Beth, is waiting with a coffee before I step outside the building.

The meeting goes about as well as expected. Thomas is sullen, glaring at his phone as I walk into his office unannounced. I never replied to his message. He hates being caught off-guard almost as much as he hates being disappointed. Today, I get to accomplish both.

"Son," he greets me with just the tiniest nod of the head. "What have you learned so far?" His lips form a thin line as he gives me a once-over. The room is dark for the early morning. The curtains are drawn. The fireplace simmers behind his large desk, but the light is dying, as if it's been burning for hours.

He doesn't look well. The once subtle wrinkles around his mouth are more prominent on his dry skin. Dark circles accentuate his bloodshot eyes. He's definitely not slept. He'll be less understanding than normal.

"Nothing we didn't know already. There are three attorneys working on it. They could be done by early next week." I stand near the door. I lean against the wall, my ankles crossed, displaying the nonchalance I hope will divert my father's attention away from the topic of Meghan and on to anything else.

"Do you have a plan?"

"I'm working on one."

"Fucking hell. They can't find anything, Shane," he says as if he's reminding me. "This isn't some low-stakes deal. This is critical. So you better figure something out. For fucks sake, make sure they don't find those contracts."

"I'm working on it," I say. Obviously, I'm working on it. He should trust me to do my job, or he shouldn't give me things to do. I can't be babysat the entire time I'm working.

"Press harder. Use the target. Eliminate her, for all I care. Take out the whole goddamn team. We can't afford for this to go wrong." He slams his hands on the desk. The loose pens scatter.

I shake my head. I knew he'd try this. I came prepared. "She's not an important piece. Removing her will do nothing to improve our chances."

My father leans forward so I can see him. His cruel, wrinkled face looks so much like mine. Like a mirror that cautions me about what lies ahead should I choose to continue down this path. The only difference between us is time.

"I just need a few more weeks," I explain. I push off the wall and step closer. If I can remain calm, I can talk him out of this.

"You've had time. I'm running out of patience. We tried your way. Either you end this, or I will." He jabs a finger in the air.

I grind my jaw. There's got to be some other way.

My father sighs. He places his thick hand on the desk. His silver rings thudding against the wood. "Son, I understand your hesitancy. She might be an innocent casualty. It's unfortunate. I don't relish your position. But the job must be done."

If I didn't know my father better, I might think he cared. But he only reserves this voice for manipulation. I steel myself. I won't be able to save her if I can't think critically. And I can't think critically when her safety is all I think about anymore.

"I'll go after someone else. One of the others. They're just as important, if not more so. She's point by default. She doesn't actually show up that way. Either of the others will do. Kennedy might even be better." The lie comes easily.

My father sighs louder. He pushes back from the desk, and the chair scrapes against the hardwood floor. "I hoped it wouldn't come to this," he says. He takes a manilla folder from the boxes behind him and slides it toward me. "But I had my suspicions about your . . . judgment."

I stare at the folder as if it'll disappear the longer I refuse to acknowledge its existence. I know what this is. It's her death sentence.

"Open it."

I cross the space remaining and snatch the folder off of the desk. I slip open the metal clasp, taking out a neat stack of papers as my father speaks again.

"You've been hiding this from me. An easy out." Disappointment colors his voice.

My eyes scan the papers. Her rehab records. I knew about them, but how did he get these? I'm fucked. My plan to keep her is fucked. I can't let him do this. There has to be another way.

"No," I say eventually. My mind can't come up with a solution, but I know I won't use these against her. I don't care if that shows my hand. I want to keep her safe, so I'll have to find another way to do it.

"You don't have a choice. I gave you a shot . . . that's more than I offer anyone else. But you failed. If we let this go on, they'll find what they need to call off the deal. I tried your way, son. I really did. Now we do it my way." He stands at the edge of the desk, towering above me. My father's presence is the only one capable of making me feel small. "She's just a girl, Shane. There's plenty more."

"I won't do it," I say. It's as much for her as it is for me. I need to convince myself of what I'll do next. My mind races. There's only so many ways this can play out and keep her in my life.

My father laughs. His head back, and his hand across his chest as if I told him the funniest joke. "Have you lost your goddamn mind, son? You don't have a choice." And just like that, the humor slips off his face. His black eyes ready to burn me alive. "Either you do it, or Marcus will." He juts his thumb toward my cousin, the armed guard in the corner.

I consider Marcus. His skeleton-like hands are folded neatly in front of him. The thought of that cold, calloused grip on Meghan's soft skin makes me see red.

"Fine," I say. "I'll do it." But I'll have to resort to the most undesirable of my strategies."

"Before the start of the week," he cuts me off.

My hands dig into the back of the chair I stand next to, and my body shakes from the anger that trembles within me. I consider speaking, then rethink it. Anything else I say might give away my plan, and the last thing I need is for Meghan to end up even more on my father's radar.

I leave without another word. In the minutes this conversation took, I've come to a realization. I'll do whatever it takes to keep her safe. Even if that makes her hate me.

Chapter Fifteen: Meghan

The apartment gets dark more quickly at this time of year. The large glass windows overlooking the neighborhood cast shadows across the room that I don't bother to light. Mina weaves in and out of my legs as I walk to the bedroom. Her tail flickers against me as I try to avoid the corners of the furniture. She's impatient. She loves our nightly routine. It's nearly past midnight so we should've been in bed by now. As if reading my thoughts, she meows loudly. I promised I wouldn't stay up working all night, and here we are. Another Saturday night I lost to legal documents and my laptop screen.

I wonder when I'll stop working instead of living.

I don't bother to turn the light on in the bedroom either. Not even the TV. If I have to look at another screen, I'll break. Not that I could see it anyway. I took my contacts out for the night and left my glasses in the living room. My best attempt at counteracting my desire to work more.

My phone rings, and my heart beats faster. It's not until I read Kennedy's name that I realize the excitement was in hoping he would finally call.

"Hi," I say. I pull the covers up around my waist. I don't know why I fantasized about an apology. He's clearly not the type.

"Hey," she singsongs. The background noise from wherever she is thuds loudly. "You wanna come out?"

"No, thanks, I'm already in bed."

"Boo, are you sure?"

"Yeah, I have a lot of work to get through still before Monday, so I need to get some sleep while I can."

"Even if Shane is here?"

My heart beats faster. "Why would I care about that?" I think about the way it felt when he touched me. I think about the way he looked at me. About the jacket he let me wear, then keep. The jacket I let myself fall asleep in last night. The jacket curled up into a ball next to me like some teddy bear I'm about to snuggle up with.

"Oh, come off it. He's been looking around the room all night. Tell me that's not for you."

"Ken, no. You don't understand. He's not interested in me." He's just an almost-nice man who took me home and made sure I was safe and warm.

"I don't know. Sophia's been all over him all night, and he's not even blinked in her direction. But he practically ran after you last night."

"It doesn't mean what you think it does."

"Oh, come on, Meghan. He's perfect for you. He's got that whole dark, brooding e-boy vibe going on right now that you love so much."

"Believe me, he's the worst possible thing for me." I twist the loose strands of my hair.

"You can't know that."

"I don't know, Ken," I start to say, and then I pause to think. She could be right. He said he just wanted to keep me safe, and then he left. And he's left me alone all day. Not exactly the signs of a predator. Not even half of the red flags I'm used to willingly ignoring.

"Just consider it. Don't shut him down before you give him a chance. He's not Andrew . . ." her voice trails off.

We don't talk about what happened with Andrew. I don't talk about it with anyone. If I pretend like it never happened, I can make the memory go away.

"Okay," I say to avoid the heavy silence. "Okay, if he makes a move, I'll give him a chance. But I'm not putting myself out there just to be rejected."

"I'm gonna go tell him that."

"Ken, no. Don't."

"What? I can't hear you."

"Kennedy, no. Please don't." That's all I can say before the line disconnects. I look at my phone. I can't believe she hung up on me.

Mina jumps into bed and curls up on her pillow next to mine. We lie like that until I can't stare at the ceiling any longer. I can usually fall asleep right away. Not tonight, though. My mind is racing, not just about Kennedy. No, I'm not really worried about her. She's harmless. Probably too drunk already to remember our conversation, let alone relay it to Shane. No, it's the regret that takes hold sometimes at night. I can't predict when it will. Its claws always exist in my mind. But the nails only dig in when I've been too safe for too long. Almost as if my subconscious wants to remind me to never grow complacent.

I roll over. I flip the pillows to find the coldest sides. I play nighttime sounds. Anything to help me relax. Anything to convince the claws to release and allow me to think of something besides Andrew.

When sleep doesn't come, I try to distract myself. I think of work. I count sheep. I try to imagine things that will steer my mind away from the worst memories of my life.

The only image that blurs out the nightmare is Shane. The thought of him pops into my mind and grows with increasing temptation until I can't resist it any longer. How dare he drag me home and make demands of me, just to ghost me all day. Is this a fucking game to him? Does he think I'm a toy he can play with?

Anger feels like the better emotion to fixate on. So I let it in.

I fill myself with outrage and venom, and it's freeing. But I want to let it out on someone else. And exhaustion makes me brave enough to do it.

I unlock my phone without a second thought and send the first thing that comes to mind.

Meghan —*What's your problem?*

His response is almost instant.

Shane —*Is there context to this question or did you want me to list everything?*

Meghan — *You attacked me in my home and then ignored me all day*

Shane —*I wouldn't consider getting you home safely an attack.*

Meghan: *Holding me against the wall is an act of aggression*

Shane —*That's not how I remember it.*

Meghan — *Then how do you remember it?*

Shane —*Just making sure my coworker got home safely.*

I'm tired of skirting around the issue. I sit up in bed. High on my sudden boldness, I ask the question I've tried to dismiss since I met him.

Meghan —*Am I not your type?*

Shane —*Don't say that.*

Meghan —*Why not?*

I press *send*. I anticipate the worst. I'm not his type. He thinks of me only as a coworker. He feels uncomfortable that I'm even asking. I've made this all up. It's pathetic to even ask.

Shane —*Because you're an angel.*

That doesn't answer my question. He's avoiding it. Which tells me everything I need to know —I'm not. He's a dick, and even he's too nice to say it to me. I'm not his type. Maybe I'll be no one's type. Maybe I'm not the kind of woman that gets a happily-ever-after.

I stare at my phone, unable to think of a response that isn't pathetic if he texts me again. I'm too old to feel sorry for myself. I've outgrown that phase of my life. I've gone to therapy. I can control my thoughts, and my thoughts will help me not feel so inadequate.

Meghan — *I don't know what that means, Shane*

Shane — *It means if you fall for me, there's no going back. So you need to fall for someone better.*

Meghan — *I think I can decide for myself*

Shane — *See, you're already defying me. Take my advice and keep your heart far away from me.*

I swallow hard. I don't know what that means, but I want to. I don't want him to push me away, either. This is the most honest conversation we've had so far, and I'm more afraid of the words stopping than of whatever meaning he's trying to convey. I'm terrified he'll slip through my fingers again, and I'll be left wondering what the strange thing is building between us.

Meghan — *No*

Shane — *No what?*

Meghan — *You don't get to decide for me*

Meghan — *I don't want to be put on some emotional pedestal and tucked away as an option*

Meghan — *At least give me the chance*

The dots appear and then fade away. Minutes pass. Then ten. And when I think he's going to ignore me the rest of the night, the dots appear again.

But I don't get to see his text. I can barely keep my eyes open and fall asleep with my phone in my hand, waiting for him to respond. My mind is no longer held captive by the nightmares of my past. Instead, it's filled with Shane. Filled with the fear that he'll reject me. And the excitement around if he doesn't. I try to stay awake. I go in and out. I want to read his response. But the heaviness of night takes hold, and eventually, I succumb to sleep.

I dream of strange things. Better than what I live through most nights. Shane looms over me like a shadow I can't escape. Not terrorizing, but always watching. His body is obscured by the shadows of large trees beneath a moonlit sky.

His arms transform into dark, twisted limbs that reach out to grab me as I try to run away. I run faster and faster, escaping down a long path, but the harder I run, the faster he is. And for some reason, I don't think I'm running away in fear. I think I want to be caught.

When I wake up suddenly, I think it's because of Mina. The sound is so familiar in the fog of interrupted sleep. She's knocked something over again. I must have forgotten to leave her food. She's so spoiled. She needs her snacks, or she gets irritable. It's not until I hear her soft meow next to me that I realize something isn't right.

By then, it's too late.

The last things I remember are the smell of *Tom Ford* cologne and a large hand covering my face before darkness overtakes me once more.

CHAPTER SIXTEEN: SHANE

Shane — *All right, Meghan. Have it your way.*
Shane — *Just remember, I warned you.*

It shouldn't have been so easy to take her. It pisses me off. Even if I'm the one who did it. *How could she be so irresponsible?* There should be someone in her life who keeps her safe. Like the fucking doorman of this overpriced apartment building.

It's easy to carry her in my arms to the elevator. I tuck her chin into my chest so it looks as if I'm bringing her home after an exciting night out. I dressed her before taking her out of her room. Not as I wanted to. I exerted self-control, slipping her slender shoulders into my jacket to hide the pjs underneath. I even put her in shoes, slinging her purse over my shoulder to complete the look. I was a gentleman. I made sure her cat had food and water and locked up behind me. I might be the villain in her story, but I'm trying not to be the monster.

My driver waits outside, just as we planned. I take her to my apartment. Which is also easier to do than it should be. My penthouse is large. Staffed by people on father's payroll. Everything is quiet by the time we make it inside. It's late. The staff is gone for the day. I'll need to get more groceries. Meghan can't live off of random scraps like I do. She deserves better. I make a note to call Ingrid in the morning and place an order.

I carry her upstairs. The guest rooms are all unmade — I don't have guests. It works well enough for me. I didn't want to put her down the hall away from my protection. Even here, I want her to be as close to me as possible. She can sleep in my bed. It's not like I'll be able to get much sleep tonight anyway.

I place her gently in the bed, slipping off her shoes and easing her arms out of the jacket before tucking her beneath the covers. She looks so peaceful. I tuck a strand of hair behind her ear. *Fuck.* Even like this, she's the most beautiful woman I've ever seen. Her face is calm and makeup-free. Her perfect cheeks are flushed, as if she's too warm. But her sleep shirt is worn to the point of becoming see-through. Her nipples are hard. The piercings tempt me. Sweet little Meghan clearly isn't so sweet. I want to slip my hand beneath her shorts to find out for certain.

But we can't start night one this way.

A twinge of guilt pokes at my consciousness for having used chloroform to knock her out. It was better than the alternative. I couldn't bring myself to drug her. My plan is to stay until she wakes. To be with her when she's confused and scared. I know that the only thing worse than fear is experiencing it alone. And Meghan never has to be alone again.

Chapter Seventeen: Meghan

The first thing I process as I wake is the pounding head-ache. Then I remember the dreams. So vivid and dark. I sit up in bed and try to find my glasses. That's when I realize nothing is right. The duvet is not my own. The bed is too big and soft. I look around. What I can make out without my glasses is all wrong. The walls are dark. This is not my room.

Terror seeps in, and I'm slow to see the figure sitting next to the bed. Shane.

"Good, you're awake," he says. He stands up and walks over to the edge of the bed, sitting down. The mattress dips beneath him. I instinctively pull the comforter up around my neck. I'm still in my pjs, a t-shirt so old it's become gauze-like, and shorts, which are as modest as most of my underwear. I don't want him to see me like this. So exposed.

"Where am I?" I ask. It's taking my brain longer to catch up with my surroundings than feels right. Almost like I've been drugged.

"You're somewhere safe," he says. His voice is closer to me. Then I feel the weight shift on the bed and feel the warmth of his skin against mine.

"Where am I," I repeat. He's too close. I pull the duvet up around my collarbones. My shirt is too thin for him to be this close to me. His smell is too overwhelming. I thought I wanted Shane, but I was wrong. I'm not ready. Not like this.

He sighs. "You're home. You're safe."

I shake my head and fight back the tears. There's some-thing not right. Did I ask him to come over somehow when I was half asleep? Did I say I wanted to see him, or did he just take me somewhere? Did he drug me? I'll fight back. I won't let him have me. No one can take things from me. Not anymore.

"This isn't my home," I start, struggling to keep my voice from breaking. "Where am I?"

"My home," he says. His voice is calm. I don't understand how he can be so calm.

"Why am I in your home?" I would never have asked him to pick me up. I wouldn't hook up with a guy in an unknown place. I'm smarter than that.

"Like I said, you're safe." He runs a hand through his tousled hair. He doesn't look like he combed it. In fact, it looks like he hasn't slept at all. The skin beneath his eyes is sunken, purple and bruise-like. Did he stay awake all night to watch me?

"Did you kidnap me?" I ask. The words are hard to get out. It sounds crazy, but there's no other explanation. I'm afraid of what he'll say. There's no normal reason to stay awake all night to watch someone sleep. Especially after taking them from their home in the middle of the night.

"It depends on how you define kidnap," he says, laughing.

He fucking laughs. I look around the room. He's definitely kidnapped me. I have no recollection. I don't know where I am. And he's fucking laughing.

"I have a life, Shane," I say. "People will know I'm missing. You need to take me back before this gets out of hand."

"You're giving demands?" His tone is unapologetic. He isn't denying it. He isn't afraid of being caught.

I think of all the crime shows I binge-watch. It's not good that he's so carefree. Criminals who plan on letting their victims go don't allow them to remember so many details. And they definitely don't allow them to see their face.

"I think you're a little past giving demands, don't you think?" He runs the back of his hand down my cheek, and I jerk away, both from the unwanted contact and from his words.

I don't know what I expected. Remorse? I change tactics. I need to appeal to whatever empathy or desire he might have. "If you let me go now, I won't tell anyone." It sounds lame, but it's true. I don't want anyone knowing. Somehow, like with Andrew, it would become my fault. My mind races with excuses that'll convince him to let me go. I decide to repeat the truth. "I swear, I won't tell anyone."

He laughs. "You think I'm worried about being caught? You really don't understand what's happening, do you?"

"I-I have a life. Work. People will know I'm missing," I say. I say it to convince myself as much as him. I'll be missed. My absence will be noticed. I have a family and a career and a nosey doorman who will notice I've not returned home. Someone will save me.

"Oh, Meghan." He strokes a finger down my face. "You don't have a job anymore, not after tomorrow." His finger trails softly down my neck then over the small part of my collarbone that's exposed. "Today, actually. It's already in motion. I couldn't stop it if I wanted to, and to be honest, I don't."

"What have you done?" My heart beats harder.

"See, I told you not to fall for me." He inches closer to me.

Without my glasses, all I can see is him. And with him so close, all I can smell is his cologne. "What have you done?" The question comes out half-choked, sounding more like a whisper. He's overwhelming my senses. I'm trapped within Shane. His larger-than-life presence is weighing down on more than just my freedom. He's all I can feel. His motive is the only thing I can work through in my mind.

"After today, you'll be put on leave, then taken off the deal. They'll still employ you, for a little while at least. But the longer you're gone, the more they'll solidify the decision they were always going to make." He strokes my face again, his eyes scanning from my eyes to my lips and back again. "They were never going to give you what you wanted, Meghan," he says more softly. "You weren't going to be happy. I did you a favor."

Of all the things Shane does to me, it's his words that hurt me most. His tongue cuts me open so his indifference can watch me bleed.

"What have you done?" I ask.

"It doesn't matter. It can't be undone. All you need to know is what I've told you." He stands.

"Why? Where are you going?" I ask as he walks away. The further he goes, the blurrier everything becomes, and the more real my fate seems. He can't leave me here. I don't want him to leave me alone almost as much as I don't want to be trapped in this room. It's not just about being taken now. I'm also afraid he'll never come back.

"I'm giving you time to process," he says.

"You hate me so much that you had to ruin my career?" I yell, making him turn around to listen to me. He doesn't just get to leave me. The blanket drops from around me, but I'm too angry to feel embarrassed.

It works. He pauses.

"I was never going to save you. I'm not the good guy, Meghan. I'll always do whatever it takes. I told you that. You might be an angel, but I'm more than willing to drag you to hell if that means I get what I want."

He walks away this time and doesn't turn back, closing the door behind him without another glance.

I hear the lock twist shut.

Minutes or hours pass before the panic attack subsides. The tears swell my eyes. The exhaustion lies heavy on my senses until I can no longer fend off sleep.

This time, I don't dream. I sleep through the night because my nightmares are saved for the day.

Chapter Eighteen: Shane

I leave Meghan in the care of my father's guards, who I trust the most. I don't like it, but it has to be done. Ingrid is in charge, with instructions to check on her every two hours, give her anything she needs, and to make sure she stays locked inside until I return. It's not ideal, but my options are limited. That's what happens when I act without a plan. I become a victim to necessity rather than the creator of my fate.

I hate this. If I abandon my work to stay with her, as I want, Meghan's relapse story could be questioned. And the half-hearted alibis I've created won't last under scrutiny long enough for me to escape before someone pieces together the truth.

I run a hand through my hair as I pretend to listen to Kennedy delegate today's tasks. There's no use. I give up my attempt to focus on work within the first ten minutes. Without Meghan, everything is dull. Yes, maintaining appearances is important, and I should be present and engaged, but I can't. I'm distracted. As I have been since I fucking met her. It's a sensation I've never experienced longer than a few minutes but now constantly sustained by this woman. I used to be focused to a fault. To the detriment of countless relationships. Meticulous in my approach to every aspect of my life. Now none of those things seem as important as getting back to Meghan.

This fucking woman. She's intoxicating. I have no way to talk to her until I get home. I should've left her phone. What the fuck is wrong with me? Do I miss her? Or do I just want to check in on what's mine? Maybe I should place a camera in the room so I can see if she's okay. The idea relaxes me. I wouldn't use it to jerk off. I'd use it to make sure she was safe.

But the thought of watching her makes me hard anyway. I start to imagine watching her undress. Her big tits bouncing as she slips the shirt up and over her body. Her stomach revealed, her hips, those thighs.

Some woman interrupts my thoughts. I don't remember her name. Laura, maybe? Or Lauren? She's the paralegal? I'm annoyed at having to pretend to listen.

"What do you want for lunch?" she asks again.

It takes a moment to process what she's said to me since all my mind can seem to focus on is what Meghan would look like as she came.

"Did you hear me?" she asks. She touches my shoulder, and that breaks me from my thoughts.

I pull back. Women only touch people when they're comfortable. I don't want her to ever feel that comfortable around me again.

"I'm fine," I say. I step away. "Thank you," I add, forcing myself to remain polite. I don't want to be friendly, but I don't want to scare her either.

"Are you sure? We're working through lunch today. We're almost done." She points to the boxes. If she notices my discomfort, she doesn't show it.

I use my good-boy smile. The one I've practiced for years. The smile I reserve for women to stop them from getting close and being hurt. Women have always been drawn to me. It doesn't make sense. It also only gets worse as I age. So I've perfected the look—handsome, approachable, but too much of a good guy to become interesting. Boring, common qualities that are desirable in everything other than a boyfriend.

"I'd like to just get through work then," I say. "I can't afford to get home late."

Chapter Nineteen: Meghan

When the door opens a few hours later, I assume it's Shane. I'm ready to fight. I know what I'll do already. I've been practicing it in my mind. I'll take the paperweight I found on the desk and throw it at his head. It's okay if I miss. I'll use that moment of distraction to escape this room.

My fingers dig into the metal of my makeshift weapon. But the person who comes in isn't Shane. She's a smaller woman with light hair swept back into a tight bun. Her face is soft and round. Her expression is kind but stern. Dressed in simple black clothes, she doesn't look like the kind of person to guard a kidnapped woman. I see no sign of weapon, no indication of violence. Against all reason, it makes me relax.

I've barely made it out of bed since Shane left. I was too afraid to move and be caught off-guard. I can't imagine what I look like. I guess I don't care. They did this to me. This woman included. She's an accomplice in this. Whether she looks nice or not. She's a part of the reason I'm being kept here.

"I'm Ingrid," she says.

I don't respond. I watch her. Her eyes crinkle as her forehead scrunches, and she looks me up and down. I'm too panicked to react to the clear look of disapproval. Like a wild animal trapped in a cage, my shoulders tense the closer she gets, my body mirroring her movements, my adrenaline ready to push me out of this bed to escape.

"Eat." She sets down a tray of food on the bed. "If you don't like the lunch options, please write in what you'd prefer." She nods her head to the cream-colored paper folded on the tray. "I'll be back in an hour." She backs away slowly, still facing me, as if she knows I'm afraid enough to attack.

"Why am I here?" I blurt out.

"It's all right. Mr. Maddison will be back soon. Eat, Miss Mayfield. You'll need the strength." I repeat her words in my head. I'll need the strength. I don't like it. She knows my name. Why is she taking care of me? Where's Shane? Is he preparing to hurt me somewhere? Is that why he's not here?

"Is he going to kill me?" I ask. Of all my questions, it's the most important.

She shakes her head. "Mr. Maddison doesn't kill women." It's all she says. There's no smile, no reassuring glance. She just closes the door behind her. Leaving me the only bit of hope I've had since waking up. Shane Maddison won't kill me because he doesn't kill women.

Of course that means he kills men. That means Shane is dangerous, and I'm being held captive by a dangerous man. And my kidnapping is so normal that this woman doesn't bat an eye at me being held in this room. She has to know. She knows enough to at least be instructed to bring me my meals to a room I'm clearly not able to leave.

I open the folded lunch menu. In the inked script, several choices are written that sound like selections from an elegant restaurant rather than an unfolding crime scene. I choose nothing. I won't eat the food of my captors. Poison would be a too easy cause of death. If they're going to hurt me, they'll have to do it themselves.

My plan is to leave the food untouched on the bed next to me. I try and close my eyes, if not to sleep, at least to pass the time. It doesn't work. My stomach rumbles. The last time I ate was lunch yesterday. I forgot to eat dinner, working on that merger.

I eye the silver tray of food. It's enough for three people.

Two different types of croissants, a plate full of eggs, waffles, syrups, and whipped butter with biscuits on the side. The food is fresh. Steam rises off the biscuits even, so I know everything was just made. My stomach rumbles again. I lift a croissant to my nose. Does poison have a smell? I turn it over between my fingers. It looks normal. She said Shane wouldn't kill me . . . I take a tiny bit and chew. I wait a few minutes. Nothing. I take another bite and wait. Nothing.

I take my chances, choosing to believe the small woman is honest and that Shane has kidnapped me for reasons other than murder. The thought should make me more afraid, but instead, I'm relieved. I'm starving. And the breakfast is delicious. I eat past the point of feeling full. The ease of one fear has only created another. This could be my last meal. He could try to use my hunger against me. Tempt me with the threat of starvation. Control me.

I finish all the food on the tray. I hate it. I hate him. I hate Ingrid, or whatever her name is.

I suppose, for a prison, I could be in worse conditions. It's the other piece of hope I start to cling to. If he's keeping me in this room, something so beautiful and plush, then maybe his plan isn't to hurt me at all. I don't know why that's so comforting. Hurt or not, I'm still kept captive. But awful things don't tend to happen in rooms like this. At least not to me in my life. Awful things always happen in the safest places.

Here, at least, I'm alone. Prisoner. But somehow, that's less terrifying with each passing minute. I do still feel fear when I think too much. But fear does little to prevent disasters. So I try to distract myself with exploring.

The room is more like a suite than a bedroom. There's the large king-sized bed I've been sleeping in across from a fireplace. Next to that is a reading nook and desk. I even have a large flat-screen TV that I initially mistook for a painting. The screen is hidden in a gilded frame that looks as if it belongs in a museum rather than in someone's home. And I have the remote. He's left me with this small connection to the outside world, at least.

But that's the only connection I'm allowed. That and Ingrid. There's no phone. The doors are locked. The windows, of course, are floor-to-ceiling, with automatic blackout curtains to keep the room as dark as needed. I'm kept here because this fucker would live in the penthouse. From this floor, I can see the entire skyline of the city. I can't escape. I have no option but to bide my time here and wait for him to reveal his plan.

It's not all bad. The small reading nook outside of the bathroom has hundreds of books to read in soft leather chairs, the most worn of all the furniture I've seen so far. The bookshelves cover the entirety of the wall, filled with leather-bound spines of classics and contemporary reads alike.

The bathroom is equally luxurious. The black marble tile is elegant, more like a spa than a bath. There's a walk-in shower and a separate soaking tub. He left me with the best shampoo, conditioner, body wash, and lotion. I wonder if he bought these just for me. The *La Mer* is still in its protective cellophane packaging. The thought that he bought small luxuries for me shouldn't be endearing. It's a sign of premeditation. But it's also the most thoughtful thing any man has ever done.

He's even laid out clothes for me to change into. As if I'd wear them. I pick up the options he left me. One of his oversized cotton t-shirts and a pair of his boxers. They smell of him. I absolutely won't be putting those on. But there's also slippers and a cashmere robe so soft I consider wearing it instead.

It's tempting to enjoy the amenities of the room. I want to shower, to wash away the dried sweat and tears. I want to curl up in soft clothing and read until my eyes grow heavy enough for sleep. But this isn't a vacation, I remind myself. This isn't cozy. This is wrong. I climb back into the bed and stare at the door, waiting for whoever is next.

Every few hours, Ingrid comes back to check on me. She brings me lunch, even though I refuse to make a selection. She brings me water, sparkling and still, and coffee. The coffee is always black, just like I told Shane I liked it.

I want to refuse all kindness, but my resolve weakens. I find a way to justify it. If he's going to kill me, he's going to kill me. Showering or not showering won't save me now. Death is death. Indulging in the small pleasures available to me won't make any of this hurt less in the end, but it will allow me some final moments of happiness. It's not giving in. It's fighting back. He can't take everything.

I come to terms with my decision. I take the small bone china cup with me to the shower and turn the water on as hot as it will go. I can't help the moan that escapes my lips as the pressure beats down on my shoulders. It's better than I thought it would feel. I stand there for minutes, unable to really move, just enjoying the feel of the water. I drink my coffee in small sips between the moments of relaxation, soaking in the heat from the steam trapped around me.

I don't move until my coffee is gone. I set the cup on the ledge and pick up the bottles of shampoo and conditioner he's left me. Everything here is the best. Why would he buy these? Is it for me? Or am I overanalyzing, hoping to find clues he'll keep me alive, when really these are just the products that he uses every day and my presence here means nothing to him.

My life means nothing to him.

I try to not think. I try to enjoy it. It's hard. The weight of my situation starts to overpower the pleasure of the shower, and I change my mind again. I can't enjoy this. I need to hurry up and get back to planning how to find a way out.

I'm just getting out of the bathroom when I hear a lock turn. I've only managed to put back on my t-shirt. It's a quick decision to ditch the towel and shorts and hide myself beneath the covers of the bed once more.

I hope for Ingrid, but it's Shane who walks through the door.

"Miss me?" he asks. He throws a phone on the bed. His dark hair is disheveled. He looks tired. But the second his eyes meet mine, his face lights up, and his lips twitch around the corners.

"No," I say. I check to make sure the duvet hides my legs.

"Well, I missed you," he says. He closes the door without locking it.

I wonder if it locks from the outside or if he just thinks he can keep me from escaping himself.

"Lucky for you I'm trapped, then," I say. I cross my arms against my chest.

"My thoughts exactly."

"Do you do this to all the girls?" I snap. "Kidnapping? Is there someone else down the hall? Will you go back and forth between the two of us, deciding neither of us is enough to get your fill?"

"I respect the boundaries a woman sets." He smirks. He mimics my posture. His arms crossed against his chest makes his shoulder muscles ripple. "Usually."

"Clearly, the epitome of Prince Charming."

"You know, I think you're more adorable when you're sarcastic."

"Are you actually insane?"

"I thought it was impossible to find you more attractive. But it seems I was mistaken." He stalks toward me like I'm his prey. His long legs cross the room in four steps.

I try to ignore the spark of excitement at the admission of his attraction to me. "Why are you doing this? What are you planning on doing with me?" I wrap the covers up around my neck as if it'll keep me safe from him.

"I don't make a habit of indulging tedious questions, but for you, I seem to make all the exceptions."

"What does that mean, Shane?" My eyes water. It's not emotion for the reasons it should be. It's tears of frustration building. Frustration at myself, for after all he's put me through, and I'm still drawn to him. I'm unstable.

"It means you're safe." His thumb brushes away a tear that falls. "From everything except me."

My bottom lip trembles and a cry escapes my chest, but its sound is cut off by the sudden press of Shane's lips against mine. He doesn't kiss me. He devours. It's like trapping me here isn't enough. He needs to suck my soul out, as well. I'm learning there's nothing gentle when it comes to Shane. Not even his affection. His tongue is brutal, dominating mine. His teeth pull and bite until I bleed.

I hate myself for loving how he feels. I can't help but moan as his fingers tangle in my hair. It urges him on. He yanks my head back to kiss my neck.

Then he pulls away.

It happens so fast I'm not ready. I don't react sensibly. I need more. The thing constricted in my chest breaks free. Without thinking, I untangle myself from the covers. I kneel, pulling his face back to mine, and kiss him. I dig my nails into his neck and shove my tongue into his mouth. At first, he's startled. It's a nice change of pace. I take that opportunity to pull him into the bed.

He obliges.

We fall back together. His arms hold him up from crushing my body. But that distance isn't what I want. I move to reposition myself on top of him. I straddle him. Our height difference is less annoying like this.

Shane doesn't stop me. If anything, he tries to overpower me. It's a kiss like I've never experienced. His tongue and teeth mash against mine with inhibition. Before, with someone else, I might have worried about not kissing well enough, but with Shane, there's no worry. It's a battle of whose passion can overtake the other.

When we finally break apart, neither of us says a word. I watch him, his chest heaving up and down, wondering if I affect him as much as he affects me.

The animalistic side of me dies beneath the return of common sense. I can't be with him. It's all wrong. I promised myself I wouldn't be taken advantage of ever again. Instead, I've exposed myself completely.

The confidence I had disappears. I try and move off of him, but he stops me. One hand grips my face while the other squeezes around my arm. His thumb digs into my cheek with such force I think it might pierce the skin. He's challenging me. Trying to get me to break and pull away, but I won't give in that easily.

We stay there, staring into each other's eyes until something flickers through his — a decision.

"All right, have it your way." His lips twist into a cruel grin.

There's something imperfect about his features. Yet all it does is make him more beautiful. His cheekbones are pronounced in this dim light, casting shadows across his face that transform him into the villain I'm so desperate not to want.

"But I can't have you attacking me again. It derails my focus. Your safe word is red."

My stomach clenches at his words. Only the hand around my arm releases. I think he'll let me go completely. Then I watch him reach into the nightstand and pull out rope. Self-preservation alarms should sound in my body. He's already kidnapped me. Locked me in a room. Adrenaline should kick in to save me. Everything about my body should be preparing to fight him off. Instead, my body pulsates at the anticipation of what he might do next.

"Repeat it. What's your safe word?"

"Red," I say.

"Good girl."

I think I'm attracted to his cruelty as much as I am to his strange beauty. So when he grabs me and pins me beneath him, the fight in my legs is only half as strong as I know I'm capable of. When I thrash around, I relish the feel of his solid grasp restraining me and the way my body grinds against his.

Shane overpowers me with ease. With one hand, he pins my arms down and ties my wrists with the other. My arms are useless above my head. That doesn't stop him from securing the knot at my wrists to the right post of the bed. He makes quick work of it, still straddling my waist so I can't move. I pray he stays there. If he moves off of my body, he'll quickly realize I have nothing on besides this shirt. That shouldn't make wetness pool between my legs, but it does. And I don't know what exactly I'm hoping he'll do.

Chapter Twenty: Shane

I should've known this seemingly innocent woman might not be so sweet after all when I saw her piercings that day in the bathroom. But lots of people can make drunk decisions or fall victim to peer pressure, and I pushed aside that little bit of information so that I could focus. I told myself it meant nothing. That pretty little Meghan wouldn't entertain the darkness within me. That she couldn't like pain.

I know better now.

Those bright green eyes never leave mine, causing my dick to twitch as she runs her teeth over her skin.

Everything about her face is so pretty and perfect that it hurts.

Then there's her body. There's nothing sweet about that. Meghan is a myth come to life, with curves and soft skin goddesses have killed for. Somehow, even dressed in that ratty threadbare t-shirt, it's the hottest thing I've ever seen. I drink in the ample curve of her tits, unable to break away from the sight of the piercings peeking through, begging me to take them in my mouth.

She narrows her eyes to glare at me when I've looked too long. I can't help but grin. It's becoming my favorite expression. It means she's about to fight back. And I love it when she fights back.

"Tell me, how did you get into bondage?" I lean forward to whisper in her ear.

Her reaction is better than I'd hoped for. First, she freezes. Then she shivers before her face drains of color as her perfect mouth pops open in surprise.

What I would give to skip all the bullshit and be able to push my dick into that soft mouth.

"I'm not into this," she says, breathless. A lie. She has a safe word, and she's not using it.

"No?" I lean back to take her all in. My dick twitches again. She's so beautiful and so clearly turned on that it hurts my chest to look too long and not touch her. Her cheeks are flushed. Her nipples are hard. I try to look at her with all the disbelief I can muster. I do enjoy the theatrics of this. Drawing out her suffering. Knowing that this tension will crescendo into the greatest release of our lives. "Your browser history would suggest differently." I hold up her phone so she can see the proof as I scroll through the names of websites.

She stutters then stops talking altogether. Her pretty eyes are wide but no longer in terror. No, instead, she looks embarrassed.

Interesting.

"It escalates." I scroll down more. "Tell me, have you always gone to extremes to find release?" While I love taunting her, I'm also desperate to know the answer. It'll tell me if this thing building between us can work.

She shakes her head and squeezes her eyes shut. The tears start falling faster.

"And then it stops altogether." I scroll to the end of her explicit browser history. There's a six-month gap between the last time she watched porn and today. "I know you didn't just delete it. Clearly, I can recover anything. So why did you stop watching? Did it stop working? Did you need to go to darker fetishes to find release? Tell me." I lean forward to grip her thighs beneath my hands. It's the only touch I allow myself. Anything more, and I'll have to fuck her before she's ready.

"I-I can't," she sobs.

"What do you mean you can't?" I ask, squeezing her flesh hard enough to redden. Surely we're past lying to each other.

Is she seeing someone? Did getting sober mean giving up sex, too? Does she not have a sex drive? No. I would've picked up on that. I think of her fuck-me eyes every time I stand next to her. She wants me. I'm not making this up.

"I can't," she cries again.

The cries frustrate me. "You can't tell me?" I don't understand.

The silence that extends between us sets me on edge. Maybe I had it all wrong. She's not the kind of woman who longs for a man like me to take away her will. *Fuck.* I run a rough palm over my face. I've stolen and tied up some woman for the sake of securing a business deal, hoping to make her body submit to me as my reward.

I'm about ready to untie her and have my driver take her back to her apartment when she speaks. It's so soft that I almost don't hear her words.

"I can't come anymore." Her head slumps to the side in defeat. "It wasn't enough. The porn. Anything I try. It's not enough. I can't come." Her lips tremble.

It takes a moment to accept she's said those words out loud, and it's not just my daydreams running away from my control. She needs more. It makes my interest ignite into absolute obsession. This perfect, sweet woman has kinks as dark as mine. It's everything I wanted. Dreamed of.

But instead of filling me with hope, it pisses me off. How can she exist only to become my assignment? Why couldn't I have met her like a normal person? Maybe then we would've had a chance. Life is never fair, but this seems especially cruel. Her body is tied up to my bed. Her soft skin begging to have my fingers dig into it and leave my mark behind. All for her to end up an assignment on my father's list. Guaranteeing her to hate me.

It's as if she was made for me. Temptation manifested in a person. Did my father put her in my path to derail my future?

Is she my failure? I run a hand through my hair. I can't turn back now. I'm too far gone. I can smell her arousal. I know if I shove my hand between her legs, I'll find those thick thighs coated in her body's beautiful reaction to me, begging me to devour her.

I'm rarely certain about the morality of my actions. I don't typically concern myself with right or wrong, only with what moves me closer to my goal. I'm not sure what my goal with Meghan is, but I know that if I don't take her now, I'll never be able to think clearly for what needs to happen next when I set her free from this room. And I can't afford to make any mistakes about her freedom.

I'm doing this for her as much as I'm doing this for me, I tell myself. She might hate me. But I know she wants this. I straddle her legs so she's utterly trapped. Her hands are still secured to the headboard, her pretty little head propped up on a pillow so she has nowhere to look but up at me.

Even though she's restrained, she fights back. Her arms pull and tug at the rope to no avail. It makes me happy to watch her. I trail my fingers over her thighs. Up and down in a relentless rhythm. I don't look away from her face. I want to savor the moment she realizes what I'm about to do.

My fingertips brush the hem of the shirt she wears like a dress, and she whimpers. Her eyes squeeze shut.

"Keep your eyes on me," I say.

"No, please, no," she cries. Her lips shake as she looks at me, pleading. Her hips attempt to scoot her back away from me, but I grasp her thighs in my hands.

I hold her down with one hand while I edge up her skin with the other.

She clamps her thighs together. My sweet girl is strong.

I dig my knee in between her legs and pry them apart. I straddle one leg so she can't escape me again.

I watch the tears fall down her face as my touch inches

upward.

Her breath catches as my fingers finally pass the hemline. I move further this time, finding no underwear. Good. She won't need those ever again. I hold her gaze as I push her thighs further apart. It's so beautiful, the fear, the anticipation, the hope. I want her to know the power I have over her, but I'm careful to not reveal the power she has over me. I could come already, just from watching her. I have to slow my movements to calm myself before continuing on. When I'm certain I've regained the self-control, I graze my fingertips from the joint of her hip and thigh to her soft cunt.

It's better than I ever imagined. I nudge her thighs apart more as I ease my way into her warmth, spreading her apart. I find her clit and circle slowly, studying her face to see what movements feel best.

"Shane, no." Her cries turn to moans as I press my thumb against her sensitive spot.

She tries to move away again.

I move my hand holding her thigh in place to her neck and squeeze. "Don't move," I say. "Or I'll make it hurt instead."

"I don't want you," she says, trying to steel herself.

But her words are lies. She doesn't say *red*. And as my hand tightens around her neck, she becomes more aroused. She's so wet. I want to spread her thighs apart and feast on her until her legs shake and clench around my face.

"I know you're lying," I say, circling her more slowly. I like antagonizing her. I get off on it. "I can feel it, baby."

"I hate you," she groans. Her head falls to the side in the pleasure she seems determined to hide from me.

I grab her chin between my thumb and finger and force her eyes back on me. I want to see every second. "I love your hate." I bend down to kiss her lips. This time, she keeps her eyes locked on me. "Good girl." I place my hand back around her neck while the other circles her clit faster.

Her pulse beats harder into my skin. "I hate you so much," she cries.

My dick is so hard it hurts.

I thrust two fingers inside of her to take back control. The surprise of my claim on her pussy works. I didn't plan on letting her finish when I started. I wanted to bring her close until she begged and moaned my name. I wanted her to plead. For tears to fall down those cheeks as her lips said my name and prayed for me to make her come. Let her come. The tenuous line between ecstasy and pain within my power alone. I planned on keeping her within that moment. Because that would be the moment that she understood she belongs to me. And I want to capture that in my memory forever.

But my plans never seem to work with Meghan.

I didn't expect her to be so responsive. It's as if she's never been properly touched. She was wet before I even slipped a single finger inside her. Now she's soaking. Her back arches off the bed. The switch in her submission coming so quickly.

"Shane, please." Her begging came so easily. Looking up at me with pleading, teary eyes that nearly make me come in my pants. Like I'm a fucking teenager. Just the sight of her near orgasm is the most beautiful thing I've ever seen.

It clouds my resolve.

"I thought you hated me?" I say the words low and harsh. She's so wet. "Hmm?" I lean closer so my breath brushes against her ear. "You hate me, don't you?" I kiss and nip at the skin on her neck still visible beneath my grasp.

She nods her head. A small moan is the only sound she can make.

"Say it. Say you hate me."

"I hate you." Her lips move, but I barely hear the words as her voice gives way to a cry for release.

So I let her come. And when she comes, oh my god, when she comes beneath my touch, clenching tightly around my fingers, saying my name like a prayer, I know I'm fucked.

She wasn't supposed to come, and neither was I. But it's too late. I need release. I leave her tied up and spent on the bed, her chest heaving as she tries to catch her breath. She's safer here. If she's near me, I'll end up fucking her, and I want to save that for when I'm a bit more composed. Meghan might've liked what I did to her just now, but if I push her past her limits, I'll break her before we can truly begin. And I can't afford that.

I kiss her forehead and leave the bed before I can change my mind. I need to shower. I need to come. Only then can I figure out what to do next.

The shower steam warms the room quickly. I know I need to make it fast so I can get back to her. Luckily, that's not going to be difficult. It feels like my dick has been hard since I took her from her apartment. I've waited nearly an entire day for release. I fist myself and close my eyes. The fantasy plays without delay. I imagine I'm still in bed, Meghan tied up beneath me, unable to escape, as I fuck her mouth and come on her pretty little face.

The relief is instant, albeit hollow. Only enough to prevent pain, not enough to feel satiated. It makes sense. After having her tight walls clench around my fingers, I doubt I'll ever find that blissful satisfaction in anything other than her body.

Just another reason to never let her go.

Chapter Twenty-One: Meghan

He makes me come harder than I've ever come in my entire life, only to leave me discarded like a used toy. Any high from the orgasm is shattered at the thought. He couldn't wait to leave me here. Alone. He had to shower me off his skin.

Embarrassment turns to self-consciousness. I wonder if he's disgusted by me because I didn't shave. It's not like I was expecting this. My ex wouldn't even touch me if I wasn't completely hairless from neck to toes. But I couldn't plan for something like this. I couldn't know that my kidnapping would lead to this. God, I'm fucked up. I wanted this. I wanted him. After everything I've been through, I still wanted him. Want him. Because I'm broken.

I cry silently, hoping it'll pass before he's back. Deep down, I knew I was never right after Andrew. After what he did, I couldn't be with men for a year. Then the men I did choose to be with made me hate myself even more. They were nice. Clean-cut. Church boys, my mom would call them. But those kinds of men are always like Andrew. At first glance, safe to the world. But underneath lie monsters, desperate to ruin because, to them, they're entitled to everything.

The desires I had never made sense. I shouldn't want bondage. Couldn't actually want to be held down. I decided the fantasy was just a way to cope with what happened, my therapist agreed. An alternative ending to something tragic I couldn't forget.

But this was nothing like being with Andrew.

Shane walks back into the room, and I can't hide my sobs in time. He catches me. He wraps the towel around his waist and climbs back into bed. I hate that seeing his body has such an effect on me. I've seen naked men before. They're all the same. Fat, thin, strong, weak, it never mattered before. I didn't really have a type. A man's body alone rarely sparked lust within me, regardless of their appearance. But nothing about Shane is like other men.

Water droplets still cling to his chest as he unties me then drags me onto his lap. Common sense makes me want to resist, but the vulnerable piece he's exposed in my heart wants to bask in the little affection being offered. I settle for going limp. I don't fight back. I don't give in. I allow myself to be moved as he sees fit. So he wraps his arms around my shoulders to hold me together.

We stay like that for minutes. I cry into his bare chest and he holds me tight, letting me process without interruption. Occasionally, he strokes my still-damp hair. After a while, my body shudders involuntarily as the tears are wrung dry.

Shane squeezes me tighter and lays us down, wrapping the duvet around our bodies. It's warm and soft and comforting, especially as he nuzzles his nose into my neck, the exact opposite of everything this situation should be.

"What's wrong?" he asks quietly.

I bury my face in his skin so he can't see my emotions. I'm tired of being vulnerable and exposed. I'm tired of him.

"Meghan, look at me. Tell me what's wrong." He nudges my head with his chin when I don't respond right away.

"I want to go home," I say. It's not entirely a lie. I can't tell him the whole truth — that I'm afraid my body was the reason he ran away. Or that I'm broken because I like what he did to me. That would be a level of pathetic beyond what I'm willing to sink to. It's bad enough to be sexually aroused by my kidnapper. To admit to worrying about his satisfaction would be the ultimate disgrace.

"Well, that's not up for negotiation." He strokes my hair like this is a normal conversation. To him, it probably is. I'm not special.

"I don't want to belong to you." I try to say it with more conviction. I'm not an object for men to use. Even if Shane feels safer than Andrew, that doesn't mean they're not the same.

"That's not on the table." He kisses my head.

I hiccup. There's no use in talking to him. He'll never give me what I want. So I'll never tell him more.

"Meghan," he scolds, saying my name like I'm in trouble when I don't respond.

"I don't want to talk about this any longer." There, more definitive. I can set rules of my own. I can still protect myself. He might be able to take my freedom from me, but he can't claim my thoughts.

"Tell me or I'll bring you to the edge of orgasm and not let you come."

I snort. I don't think he meant to add levity to the situation, but I can't help but laugh. My entire romantic history was men denying me orgasms. I don't think I'd notice the difference.

"What's so funny? You don't believe me?"

"I don't think that's the punishment you think it is." I chance a glance up at him. He watches me. His thick eyebrows raised in surprise.

"Is that a challenge?" He sounds intrigued instead of the resignation I hoped for.

"No, Shane." I sigh. I rest my cheek on his bare chest, hating how much I love the feeling. Why does everything have to be a challenge to him? Why couldn't he be a nice man who wanted to take me to dinner and a movie? We might've worked out then. Instead, he's locked me in a room. "You just can't use sex as a weapon," I explain.

"I can, and I will."

"That's sick." I lift my head to look at him again. Does he realize how fucked up he sounds? Maybe he *is* like Andrew.

"That's the only way you'll learn." He's serious.

The silence builds between us. I watch him, hoping, praying to see humanity behind those brown eyes. But I don't.

He means those words. He wants to use sex as a way to control me. Just like every man before him. The tears come back harder. It hurts more to hear him say it aloud. The brief spark of hope that our intimacy provided shatters inside my chest. There is no best-case scenario to all this. No happily-ever-after. He said he would drag me to hell, and he has. I shouldn't be surprised. He's gone to great lengths to remove me from my life. Of course it's not planned to be temporary.

Shane strokes my arm, tucking the stray pieces of hair beneath my ear as I lie back down. I stay there, afraid to move, allowing my defeat to pool on his chest. My emotion doesn't change his hold on me. If anything, he holds me tighter, probably afraid I'll break before he can get all the use out of me.

CHAPTER TWENTY-TWO: SHANE

"**D**id I upset you?" I ask after a few minutes when I can no longer lie in her silence. *What went wrong?* She didn't use the safe word. She came so good. She was happy. Satisfied. I know because I watched it happen. Then I kissed her so she knew she did well. I even went to shower instead of pushing myself deep inside her. Where did I go wrong? Did something happen while I was gone? My guards are stationed at the door. No one could get in to hurt her.

She doesn't respond. But I can feel her breathing. It's heavy, so I know she's not asleep.

I try again. "Why haven't you been able to come?" I ask. I stroke her back. Her skin is so soft, even there. I love how she feels against me. It's a travesty that she's gone so long without enjoying sex. I don't know how a woman so beautiful has gone an entire lifetime without being worshiped the way she deserves.

"I just can't," she says quietly.

"Is it just with yourself or with . . . others?" I ask. The last part is hard to say. I don't like to imagine her with anyone besides me.

"I just . . . I just can't, okay? I don't know." She sounds more frustrated by my line of questioning than she was by my aggression.

"Did they not listen? Did they not do what you wanted?" I ask. I'm not the jealous type, but of course Meghan can make me feel things I never thought possible. Knowing she didn't enjoy the sex makes it easier to talk about it. I don't have to convince myself those men didn't matter. I know they didn't.

But I want to keep making her happy. And if there's something I can do to make her feel better, I need to know.

"No. I don't know. It's never about me, you know. I was just . . . there. It's fine, don't look at me like that. There was nothing they could do that I want anyways."

"What do you mean, there was nothing they could do that you wanted?"

"Like . . . even if I told them where or how to touch me, when they did it, it didn't feel good. So I gave up."

"Could you explain it to me?" I try to ask as calmly as I can. I haven't figured out yet why she shuts down sometimes, and I don't want to say the wrong thing or make the wrong move when she's finally opening up.

She blushes. Blushes. After all I've done to her—tied her up and taken away her will—what makes her blush is talking about how she receives pleasure. "I don't know. Probably not." She sighs. Defeated. She looks defeated. Her green eyes are lined with red from tears and exhaustion. "I think I don't get turned on."

"But you did for me?" I ask, afraid. She did, right?

"Yeah, well, I wasn't exactly expecting it."

"Have you been turned on by me any other times? Or was this a one-off?"

She squirms against me.

"Meghan," I say. I can't help but smile. I feel her answer before she even says it.

"There's been other times," she almost whispers to herself.

My smug smile surely turns triumphant at her admission.

"What?" she asks. Her gaze narrows as she regains her cool affect. "It's not because of you. It's . . . situational, I don't know."

"You don't know?" I challenge. If she keeps this up, I'm gonna make her come again just to prove I can.

She stares at me, unmoving, as if unable to answer.

"You know what I think? I think it's because you like being dominated by me. You love that I took away your choice. You're desperate to be overpowered, for once in your life." I kiss her forehead.

"Are you trying to make yourself feel better about what just happened?"

"I don't need to make myself feel better. I love what just happened as much as you do. I can't wait to do it again." I grin.

"I'm never letting you do that again," she says. She rests her head back on me.

I laugh. I can hear her breathing even out. Despite what she's said, I feel her relax into my body. It's nice to just hold her. I stroke her arm, then her hair. She's perfect, every inch of her body. I would hold her forever if I could.

"Shane," she says hesitantly. "C-could I ask you a question?"

"Sure," I say. I kiss her hair. She's going to ask me if I'll let her return home. Or when I'll let her leave. I've prepared a response. I don't want her to panic. So I'll say within the week. It's true, I think. Within the week the merger will be done, and I can find a way to let her go. My father just needs the deal to go through. He doesn't need her. After next week, she'll be able to go back to her life. Or what's left of it. She's a smart woman, though. She'll find another job. And I've already planned the bank transfer to get her through the next year if she needs it. More, if she wants. Because even if I let her leave, I'll never truly let her go.

"Did my body bother you?" she asks. Her voice is so small and quiet, at first, I think I've heard her wrong.

"What?" I ask. I definitely heard her wrong.

"Did my, did my body bother you? I know I didn't shave and—"

I cut her off. "You're fine," I say. I hate that she even has to ask. I want to put a stop to that nonsense before it starts.

"Oh." She looks like she might cry again.

"No, you're fine." I squeeze her tight. "As in, you can do whatever you want, whatever makes you comfortable. I don't care either way." I mean it, I don't. Nothing would stop me from enjoying her body. I'm not an idiot. I understand she's a grown woman with a woman's body. That's the entire point.

"Oh," she says.

Shit. She still doesn't understand. How can she not understand? I roll her onto her back so I can cage her beneath me. "Your body is perfect for me, Meghan. If I could create the perfect shape, it would be yours. I promise."

"Oh." She blushes deep. Despite herself, she smiles. A small, shy smile.

"Yeah." I kiss her forehead and roll to lie on my back beside her. Fuck me. If I'm not careful, I'll get hard again, and I really don't know how long I can hold off from thrusting deep inside of her.

"Well, that doesn't change anything," she says. She sounds more like herself. "We can't do that again, okay?"

I grab her hand and lace our fingers together. "I can, and I will. That I also promise you. And I'll make sure you love every second of it."

Chapter Twenty-Three: Meghan

Shane and I stop talking because I fall asleep soon after he assures me that he loves my body. I blame the heat from his skin and the exhaustion from being unable to sleep the last few nights. And the orgasm. There's no other explanation for falling asleep in the arms of my captor, thrilled to know he approves of me.

By the time I wake up the next morning, Shane is gone. Or more likely, the lack of warmth from him leaving woke me up. It's unsettling that I find comfort in his presence. I tell myself it's because when he's with me, I know what he's planning. But that's not completely true. I didn't know he planned to touch me last night, and I took a great deal of comfort in that. I rub my thighs together at the memory.

He left me a note on his pillow. The same heavy paper as the menus from yesterday. In his childish handwriting, the note says, *I'm sorry I'm not there beside you. I hope you can forgive me. The phone is yours. Text me if you need anything.*

I find the phone on the nightstand. It's not my phone. He wouldn't leave me with mine. It's naive to hope his interest in sex is anything more than that. There's no hidden meaning in his touches. I'm just his current captive audience.

I power on the phone. It's useless. The only numbers I can call or text are preprogrammed in. Shane, obviously, although he made sure to put heart emojis next to his name. Ingrid. The house . . . I assume that's wherever I am. Security. I can't call for help or reach anyone who Shane's not pre-approved. The man thinks of everything.

I don't text him. I decide I actually never want to talk to him again. Every time I think of him, I'm overcome with shame. I can't believe I came from just his fingers. Not even my own fingers make me feel the way he did. Surely it was a lucky accident. He can't actually know my body better than I do. It wasn't desire I felt. It was a delusion. I went too long without sex. He's not special, I'm just horny, so it's normal to replay last night. The way he took control of me, how he touched me as if he knew exactly what would feel good and when I would come. How it made me feel safe.

I wish I could say this morning apart was helping me come to my senses. But a part of me wishes he'd come back here and try again. I might say *red*. I'd definitely say *red*, as long as I didn't look him in the eyes. Or feel his body against mine. Or hear his voice whisper commands in my ear. Yet every time the door opens and Ingrid walks through, a pang of disappointment washes over me. Not Shane, my body thinks. I want Shane. My body and my mind are at odds, however. I ignore his text messages. Dismiss his call around lunchtime. I'm at a crossroads. If I give into this, there's no painless way out. I need a way out.

Replay quickly becomes rumination. Within the confines of this room, there's only so many options. I can give into the addictive nature of my thoughts. I can shower, or watch TV, and I do. All of which only distracts me from my reality for minutes at a time. When those things no longer work, I give up and try escapism. The wall full of books offers me hope on a day that desperately needs it. Reluctantly, I put on the clothes and cashmere robe he's left for me and curl up in one of the leather chairs with an arm full of books.

I hate that he knows me so well, even in this. The things I refused to wear now comfort my body. The prison he's left me in creates a home. The lust I've pushed down burns me alive.

I set my stack on the table next to me and lose myself in stories until my eyes ache from the strain of reading.

Initially, I don't hear when Shane comes home. I feel him. He stands over me like a shadow I can't escape. Truly, I can't. He's permanently following me.

He's permanently following me, eclipsing any light from my life, every opportunity he gets.

"What are you reading?" he asks.

I make note of the page I'm on and shut the book in my lap. "Poe." I stand so he can't tower over me quite so much. I don't like the advantage he has. Everything he does makes me feel small. It's not a feeling I'm used to. I'm always in charge. I'm the person people look to for direction. I hold the power in any dynamic.

Not with Shane.

"You do seem to gravitate toward the macabre," he says.

"You would like that, wouldn't you. Make the whole villainous pervert thing more forgivable." I sidestep him before he can back me into any walls. I try to slip away by rounding the corner to the bathroom where I can lock him out, but I walk right into the table. Pain sears my thigh.

"It's hardly my fault. You make it so easy to be taken."

My clumsiness allows him the opportunity to back me into the bookshelf and press his body against mine.

"It'd be harder to take me if I could see, ya know. You took me without my glasses. You took me without anything."

"Would you like me to bring them to you?" he asks, as if my stuff is simply down the hall.

"I'd like you to let me go," I snap.

"Well, that can't happen. Not yet. So what would you like brought here . . . to make you more comfortable."

I fixate on the *not yet*. There's a chance.

"Give me a list, Meghan, or I'll have your entire apartment

moved here." He narrows his eyes.

"You wouldn't."

"Try me."

"Fine. Let me think." There're so many things I need. "Give me some space so I can think better." I push against his chest.

He chuckles but steps back.

"My glasses, my face wash, actually my entire makeup bag, the pink one. There's a face cream I need, too. It should be on the shelf next to the pink bag. My cat, obviously. And everything she needs. Oh, and some change of clothes that's more comfortable."

Shane pinches the bridge of his nose, and I think my plan has worked. He says he won't kill me, so my best bet is to annoy him until he decides I'm not worth the effort.

"Oh, and my anxiety medicine. I don't remember where that is, though. It could be in my briefcase, but you'll also need to check the medicine cabinet, or sometimes I . . ."

Shane lunges down and captures my lips in his before I can finish my sentence. His mouth moves slowly, the touch so unlike last night. He keeps a hand on my hip. The other snakes into my hair as his tongue slides against mine. His hold is gentle. He presses my back against the shelving once more. I hear a few books tumble to the floor as he pushes into me, but the sound isn't enough to break us apart.

I can feel his erection hard against my stomach. I wish I could say that made me flinch in disgust, but it makes me cling to him more.

"I'll get you whatever you need. Text me the details so I can forward it to Ingrid."

"You're not going to go get it?" I ask.

"No, I have other plans for us." He kisses my forehead and walks into the bathroom. "Come on," he says, holding out his hand expectantly. He waits for me to follow, then closes the door behind us.

Chapter Twenty-Four: Meghan

Shane starts to undress, and I try not to watch. I stare at my toes. His shirt hits the floor. I study my chipped pink nail polish and think of all the appointments I'll need to reschedule when I return to my life because I *will* get to return to my life. His pants thud softly against the cold marble from the weight of his belt. My thoughts stall out. *Shit.* His boxers fall next. *Shit, shit, shit.*

He places two fingers beneath my chin and lifts my face.

My heart starts to thud like it wants to break free of my chest. I let his fingers guide my jaw, but I squeeze my eyes shut as he does. I can't look at him. If I look at him, I'll lose any sense of rationale I have left.

"Meghan," he chides. "I want to see your eyes."

"Why?" I shift back and forth. This is too much. I keep my eyes closed. I need to leave.

"Because they're beautiful. And they tell me how you feel when your words won't."

"Shane, I don't want to do this." I can't do this. I feel like I'm going to hyperventilate from the pressure on my lungs.

"Why?" he asks.

"I just don't want to." Fuck, I say it as I look up at him and immediately regret it. He's completely naked. His broad shoulders extend into lean, muscular arms that I desperately want to feel wrapped around my body. His chest is perfect, but I knew that already. My head is constantly pressed against it any time he holds me. But his torso takes me by surprise. I don't understand how I'm so attracted to a man's waist. My mouth practically salivates as my eyes sweep down. It narrows into a v-line I can't look away from. *God.* He's beautiful. And that beautiful line extends and draws my eyes to what I've tried to pretend didn't exist, his dick. It's hard, thick, and the biggest I've ever seen.

"Give me a good reason why, and I'll stop." He steps closer. His dick jerks slightly as he stares at me.

I can't think of a response. I can only admire him.

"C'mon, before I lose my patience." He pulls me against him and kisses down my neck. He presses himself into me until I can feel every inch of his hard length.

I'm not getting naked in front of this man.

"Meghan," he warns.

"I-I don't want you to look at me." I turn my cheek so he can't see my expression as I say it.

"Not a good enough reason." He trails kisses over my collarbone. His hands slip down the small of my back to grab my ass. Shane's hands are large, but even his hands aren't large enough to grasp me entirely. His fingers stretch out and dig into my flesh.

"It's a great reason. I don't want you to see me like this."

"I've already seen you." His kisses turn to soft bites that send goosebumps down my arms.

"In dim lighting, not like this." I need to keep myself together. I can't give in.

"It's the same thing."

"I'll disgust you. I'm too . . . big for you."

He stops nipping at my skin and pushes me back slightly to hold me at arm's length. He looks at me as if waiting for the punchline. When I don't laugh, he looks concerned. "You're serious? I'm like a foot taller than you . . ." The way his voice trails off makes it sound like he's beginning to question my sanity.

"No, not height. I'm not little. I'm not going to look good

like this, in here. I'm not the type of girl you can pick up and fuck in the shower." I look around the room. Or the counter. I cringe at the thought of him trying to lift me up.

He looks me up and down. "Do you think I don't know what you look like? Hmm?"

"W-what?"

"Do you think you're invisible?"

I shake my head. "I don't understand."

"Do you think when I get hard because of you"—he presses his length into my stomach—"it's because of your charming personality?"

"Shane, stop. This isn't the time to make jokes." I try to escape his hold on me. I don't like him looking at me while he says these things. I certainly don't want to feel him lose his hard-on when I slip off my fucking clothes.

"Why? You're clearly joking." His fingers grip me harder.

"No, I'm serious. I'm . . . sturdy." I look at the wall just behind his head as I say it, determined not to look at him.

"Holy fuck, are you serious? Who hurt you?" His eyes widen.

"What? No one. I know what I look like." I smack his hand away from my face as he tries to touch me. If he's too affectionate now, I'll mistake it for something more, and that will make me cry, and I'm not going to have this conversation and then cry in front of him. "I'm not the kind of woman you want. Not like this."

"You're exactly the kind of woman I want." The hand I smacked slips beneath the t-shirt. "This is exactly what I want." He moves both hands over my hips and waist, down over my stomach, and back up again.

I want to shrink away or suck everything in and find some way to disappear completely. I don't want him to touch me. Not like before, when I was afraid of falling for him. Now I don't want him to touch me because I don't want to watch the disappointment flash in his eyes when he feels something he doesn't like.

"Meghan, trust me," he says.

I shake my head. I can't trust him. I will not cry.

Of course he doesn't listen. He eases the shirt up my body.

I tense. This can't be happening. I know I need to stop him, but I'm frozen in place.

"Relax, you're so beautiful. Lift up your arms."

Against my better judgment, the soothing baritone of his voice makes me do as I'm told.

He stares at me. The silence in between the shirt falling to the floor and the sound of his breathing hitching in his chest makes me want to implode from embarrassment.

"You're so fucking perfect." The words come out like a whisper.

I look up at him.

He stares down at me in wonder. He runs his hands over my hips. "God, you're so fucking perfect." He moves his hands over my waist, across my stomach, over my back. He pulls me flush against him. My breasts pressing into his skin. His erection against me.

He kisses me. One of his hands grips my ass, and the other encases the small of my back. He keeps me tight against him. I can feel everything, so I know he can, too. He only releases my lips to say, "You're a fucking goddess."

"You're not going to fuck me in the shower, right?" I shift uncomfortably. I still hate being exposed. I imagine him struggling to lift my thighs around him, and it makes me want to die.

"I could if I wanted to." He looks at me sternly. "But I think shower sex is overrated. It's harder to restrain you if you're all slippery." His lips lift into a smile. "C'mon. I just want to take care of you."

I look at him skeptically.

Shane doesn't wait for me to follow. He steps into the shower and turns on the water. Steam rises around us. The drops from the waterfall showerheads cascade down. He tips his head back and lets the water run over his face. He runs a hand over his slicked-back hair and dries his eyes. "Come on," he says. He holds out a hand to help me in.

I consider my options. He's at a disadvantage now. I could use this moment to run away and beg for help. As if reading my thoughts, he cocks an eyebrow. I sigh. There's no use. He'll always catch me.

I step in, and Shane groans in approval as the water falls over my skin. He holds out his arms, and I step inside his embrace. I hate to admit it, but it feels good. He feels safe, even like this, even when I'm exposed. I snort. I'm going crazy.

We stay like that for a while, holding onto each other like the second we pull apart, the world might slip away. Then he lifts my chin. I close my eyes as the water falls over my hair and face, and I feel his hands graze over my head, then feel his fingers massage shampoo into my scalp. It feels so good. I lean my forehead into his chest as his fingertips press into me. His thumbs take extra care to circle against my temples before he eases my head back once more to rinse out the soap. He does the same for the conditioner. His fingers lavish every touch of my skin. The pressure of his attention is so beyond intimate it borders upon bliss.

Just when I think things can't get more romantic, Shane gets out of the shower first so he can dry me off with a big fluffy towel. He wraps it around my shoulders so I'm cocooned in warmth and trapped in his arms.

He tugs on my wet hair.

"Stop it," I say, but it comes out playful.

"You liked it, didn't you?" He pulls my hair again. This time, he keeps it wrapped around his hand to expose my neck. His grasp on me grows harsher. The strength from his pull causes my scalp to scream as it tries to resist.

I mean to command him to stop, but the only sound I can make is a moan as he pulls harder.

"You're such a good girl." He kisses my neck, then bites and repeats his way along my shoulder.

I shiver as the pain ebbs into ecstasy.

"My good girl likes when it hurts." He reaches into the towel to pinch a nipple between his fingers. He pinches and rubs my nipples again, while the other hand is wrapped around my hair, keeping my head back as he bites and sucks my neck. I can feel that he's getting harder.

"Shane," I moan.

"Does the pain make you wet, Meghan?" There's sadism in his eyes.

My core clenches.

Chapter Twenty-Five: Shane

"So you like when I do this. You like pain. What else do you like?" I hold her. It's nice, because she can't fight back while restrained. It's a different approach to trap her arms in a soft, warm towel instead of ropes, but with her, I like it.

"I don't know," she says.

"You don't have to be shy with me." I say the words politely instead of stating the obvious. Someone as smart and charming and beautiful as her can and have fucked whoever they want. It'd make me homicidal with jealousy if she wasn't trapped in my hands.

"Shut up, Shane. I clearly don't have the same understanding of my sexuality as you do."

She's too annoyed with me to be lying. I can see the truth of what she says in the way she purses her lips and narrows her eyes. Still, it's unexpected.

"So let's change that. What are you into?" I ask again. I know the little bit her browser history has told me. I want to know more, though. I want her to tell me how and where to touch her to erase the memory of any other men from her mind.

She shakes her head and doesn't speak. I'm starting to hate her silences.

"We have to pass the time here somehow," I say. And that time should be spent worshiping her body.

"Or you could just let me go."

I want to grab her by the throat and choke her until her resistance goes slack. Then fuck her until she begs me to let her come. But Ingrid will be back within the hour with her list. That doesn't give me enough time to enjoy her.

"Why did you stop?" I ask instead. Understanding her better is almost as good as edging her to tears.

"Stop what?" She looks at me, confused. Her tiny forehead is scrunched together. It makes me want to kiss her.

"Exploring your sexuality," I say.

She's quiet for so long that I don't think she'll respond. "I couldn't keep watching those videos ... it seemed ... it seemed wrong."

"What do you mean, wrong?" She doesn't need to be embarrassed, not in front of me. There won't be any energy left for porn when I'm done with her, but she should be honest about what she likes. I can make it come true. Better than she ever imagined.

She sighs deeply. "You wouldn't understand." She shifts her weight back and forth.

"No, really, I'm interested. I'm not trying to judge you. I want to understand you better."

She's quiet again for a while before saying, "I didn't used to watch it. Porn. I started after, after a bad break-up. I couldn't really be intimate with anyone for a while ... something happened ... so I just wanted to, you know, take care of myself. But I couldn't just watch the normal things. And you know. It escalated."

"And that made it hard to come with someone else?" I ask. Who people fuck before me has nothing to do with my worth. But Meghan and anyone else together, naked, intimate, even if it only exists in my mind, is enough to make me want to lock her back up and throw away the key.

"No, not that. I've never really been able to come with someone else. And I guess watching porn made me realize what I was into? But I couldn't try that with someone else. And watching porn stopped working. It's violent and misogynistic. I felt like I was a part of the problem, sure. But it wasn't even that. I was disgusted with myself. I wanted to be those girls so badly. I wanted someone to dominate me. I needed it to actually be *me* in order to feel something."

"And now it is you." She might not like how we started, but she can't deny the pleasure I've created in her life. Eventually, she'll give in. That'll buy me time. I need time to prove I won't hurt her. At least not in the way she's afraid of.

"And now it is. And I was right." She sounds horrified.

"Why does it sound like that makes you mad?"

"Because I'm so fucked up." She looks up at me with glassy green eyes.

"You're not fucked up."

"I am. You don't even know. How could I want this? I shouldn't want this."

"You should want whatever makes you feel good."

She shakes her head.

"I could prove it to you, you know. I could help you explore all that. Just say the word." I kiss her. "Or don't. Your kink is being dominated. Mine is taking you whenever I want." My dick ticks as I say it.

"That's the problem, Shane. I can't like that."

"Why not?" I ask.

She doesn't respond.

"Why not?" I really hate it when she doesn't talk to me.

She takes a deep breath. "An ex assaulted me."

The silence rings in my ears. I forget to respond and jump into planning his murder. This is my skill set. In the family business, I'm the enforcer. The strategist that keeps assignments safe and targets from creating problems we can't afford to exist. Meghan is my assignment, now to protect. So I'll kill him. I'll kill anyone that hurts her.

"What's his name?" The words are staccato and strained.

"W-what?" she asks.

"What's. His. Name."

"Andrew."

"Andrew-what?" I snap. I'm going to slit his throat and watch him drown in his own blood.

"Andrew Knight."

I hold her tighter to me and take a grounding breath. "I will never hurt you like that, Meghan. I swear." I kiss her head. Twice. She needs to understand when I mean to take things from her, I'll always return something even greater. She'll never be empty because of me. She'll never have to be empty again.

I untangle myself from her. My plans for her body can wait. Tonight, I need to take care of her heart.

"Come on," I say more calmly, shoving the darker part of my desires down. "Let's tuck you into bed, sweet girl. I want you to get some sleep."

Chapter Twenty-Six: Meghan

Shane tries to distract me. He dresses me in his clothes and literally tucks me into bed, taking care to trap every inch of me within a blanket, even though it's barely nightfall. The moment I told him about Andrew, I knew something was off. His entire demeanor changed. And whether he wants to admit to it or not, he can't hide the shift in energy when he doesn't get beneath the covers with me. Instead, he gets dressed in black sweats and a black hoodie and climbs in next to me, lying on top of the duvet. He does his best to look normal. I hear his heartbeat slow as he turns on the TV and prattles on about inconsequential topics we've never bothered to pretend to discuss before.

The acting can only last so long. I see the strain of his unspoken emotion slip through his façade. Occasionally, his jaw flexes when his eyes stray to the phone screen he keeps hidden by his side. It's as if he's waiting on something. And the ping of a notification confirms it.

He strokes my hair one last time before kissing my forehead. "I'll be back soon. Try and go to sleep."

I know he's lying, but I don't press him for the truth. A part of me knows already and is eager for details. Another part of me is just desperate to forget. I compromise with myself and lose my consciousness to reality TV. I'm not sure what part of rich housewives' fake fighting is meditative, but it soothes my tangled thoughts and allows me a moment of peace, even if it's brief.

When the door creeks open a while later, I assume it's

Shane. He's been gone for well over an hour, and as embarrassing as it is to admit, it's hard to sleep without him. I don't like waiting, I tell myself. It's not that I like sleeping next to him. It's that I need to know where he went.

But the figure in the doorway isn't Shane. It's Ingrid. She flips on the light and enters with a suitcase full of my things, Mina in her carrier, and two large people ushering in bags that look like they're from a department store.

"Where would you like the things?" one of them asks.

I think to respond when Ingrid answers for me. "Place the clothing in the closet. Don't bother hanging it up. I'll have someone put it away tomorrow. Set the cat up with food, water, and a litter box in the bathroom for now. We'll figure the rest out later."

The strangers shuffle around the room while Ingrid watches with her arms crossed against her chest. When she's satisfied, she offers them a stiff nod, dismissing them from the room. Only when they're gone does she acknowledge I do, in fact, exist.

"Would you like Mina with you?" she asks.

"S-sure," I say. I sit up slightly. Shane must have remembered her name. Something in my chest swells.

Ingrid releases the lock on the carrier and croons as Mina pads out, stretching before blinking slowly and offering her a soft meow. She's not afraid. She hasn't been hurt. Ingrid smiles at her, lifting her gently into her arms and carrying her over to the bed.

"She's been very good," Ingrid says, handing her to me.

I hold her tight to my chest and kiss her soft head.

"Mr. Maddison left her with food and water before bringing you here," she adds. Her eyes flick up and down my face as if searching for something. "He's sent someone over every day to check on this . . . cat."

I don't know how to respond, so I say nothing instead.

Mina purrs against my chest, and I hold her tighter.

"I've let him know your things have been delivered. Get some rest." This time, she doesn't wait for me to respond. She walks to the door without a backward glance, shutting off the light, and twisting the lock.

Chapter Twenty-Seven: Meghan

When I wake up the next morning, Shane is back. He looks so unaffected I have to remind myself that he slipped away in the middle of the night to do God knows what. There's nothing obvious in his appearance. I don't know what I expected. Blood, maybe. Or sweat dripping down his face and the weapon still clutched in his hands. Instead, he's composed. But there is something in his hand. He smiles as I realize it and hands me my cup of coffee.

"Good morning," he says. "Did you sleep well?"

"Where did you go?" I ask, sitting up.

He sighs. "Do you really want to know, Meghan?"

"Yes." I take a long sip of my coffee. It's warm and bold and soothes my chest as I drink it.

"It would make you an accomplice." He raises an eyebrow.

"Jesus, Shane, what did you do?"

"I said I would take care of you. I meant it. You have no one to be afraid of."

"Besides you," I amend.

"Besides me." He smiles.

That shouldn't make me feel better, but it does. Ingrid's words echo in my mind. He doesn't kill women. Surely, a dramatization of what he's capable of. Shane wouldn't kill someone just because I said they assaulted me years ago, right?

The thought makes me shiver. He kidnapped me and hurt someone else. I should want to go to the police. I should be desperate to escape . . . and yet, I'm not.

"Let's not talk about gruesome matters over breakfast."

Mina jumps up on the bed and pads her way between us.

"Are you going to get caught?" I don't care, I tell myself. I need to know so that I'm prepared. It'll tell me if I need to keep planning my escape or if the solution will come to me.

"I'm a professional, Meghan. This is who I am. I would never do anything illegal that I thought I would be caught doing."

Oh. My heart sinks. He doesn't think he'll be caught for me then, either. So no one knows I'm missing. And no one is coming to save me. This is who Shane really is. This is what he does for a living. "You're never going to let me go," I say. It's not a question.

"When I'm done with you, you won't want to leave." He kisses me. "But let's talk about something different. Let's talk about how this cat is not staying in the room." Shane leans back and crosses his arms against his chest. "It can stay in a spare bedroom."

"Her name is Mina," I say. I scoop her in my arms like a baby, and she purrs. I kiss her head. "I won't stay here without her. If you're going to keep me, you're keeping her. We sleep together every night."

"And now you sleep with me."

"No," I say.

"No?"

"If I'm staying, then Mina is staying."

He looks at me as if trying to find the weakness in my demand, but I refuse to be without her a second longer.

"What are you doing to me? It's impossible to say no to you." He strokes my face. "You're like a siren. I'm starting to think I won't escape your spell."

I shouldn't love his words or be impressed by his small gestures. I shouldn't care for him when he went out of his way to not care for me. Except with every compliment, every small act, I'm less and less convinced that this is a façade. I'm starting to believe he wants me.

Shane kisses my head, then yawns as he heads toward the bathroom. I hear the shower turn on. He must've spent the entire night out. I half expect him to come out and crawl back into bed with me, but when the shower turns off, he doesn't walk back into the room. Minutes pass before he emerges, dressed in a suit. He straightens the cuff on his sleeves as he walks over to me.

"Have a good day," he says. He cups my chin and places a soft kiss on my nose. He's so fucking handsome. His dark hair is still wet and disheveled across his forehead. His face is freshly shaven. His lips curve into a sly smile as he sees me drooling over him in his unbuttoned, crisp white shirt. He fastens it slowly in front of me, exaggerating the movements of his long fingers. "Try not to miss me," he murmurs.

When he leaves, he leaves the door partly open and very clearly unlocked. I don't know if this is a test. I don't even know if I want to leave. I'm uncertain about the world that awaits me outside of this room. Surely he wouldn't just let me go so easily. Are there guards stationed, ready to drag me back in here?

I take tentative steps. There's no one there. This is the first time I've dared to leave, and it creates a warm, sickly fog my body can't escape. I don't want to get caught. I don't want to make him mad. He hasn't hurt me yet, but that doesn't mean he can't or he won't. My heart hammers in my chest with each careful step. I try to keep my feet light and my movements steady. The hallway is long. The warm lighting casts soft shadows along the walls. Every second convinces me I'm inching closer to my capture, but as I make it to the landing, there's no one to be found. The upstairs is silent. I pass several bedrooms, seemingly untouched and smaller. If this is really his home, then he's kept me in his bedroom.

I don't know what to make of that.

I take the stairs, hoping to find Ingrid in the kitchen. A man I don't know is at the stove cooking eggs. My confidence catches in my throat, and I'm ready to turn around when he calls after me.

"Good morning, miss," he says loud enough for me to hear. "Your breakfast will be done soon. You may sit whenever you like."

"T-thank you," I stammer.

The kitchen is beautiful, sleek, and modern. My legs tremble as I take the final steps into the open concept.

"Mr. Maddison says you prefer your coffee black? I'll make you a cup while you wait."

I watch him carefully. The chef is a small man. The white apron tied around his plump waist suggests he truly means what he says, that he's preparing my breakfast and not a murder for hire.

I take a seat at the bar that divides the kitchen from the living room. Mina explores, too. I hear her feet pad across the floor. I watch her sniff things, then move on before she finds a stack of papers in the living room to sit on.

I wonder how long he'll keep me here. Maybe forever. I twist back and forth in my seat. The notion doesn't frighten me like it should. What will be left of my life when I go back? Do my parents miss me? Have my friends even noticed?

A pang of disappointment rings through me. My parents are busy with the election, and my friends are busy with work. It would take months for anyone in my life to realize I'm gone. That's probably why my relationship with Mina is the one I missed most. With her here, I don't miss much about my life. My bed, maybe. I think my bed is better than Shane's. I miss yoga class on Sunday mornings. I miss walking to get coffee. Besides that, I'm not sure I miss much else.

I'm nearly thirty years old, already trapped by a life I don't want to live.

I clear my throat of emotion. "I'm sorry, I'll actually take my breakfast in the room," I say. I'm too ashamed to face the world outside that door. It light is too strong to ignore the reflection of a life I no longer wish to have. I'm disgusted with myself — my contentment to stay here, hidden away, ignoring my problems.

I never wanted to face my life. The disappointment that I'd become. Maybe I can use this to my advantage. Maybe this is a great opportunity to make that pain disappear for good.

Chapter Twenty-Eight: Shane

As I leave work for lunch with my father, I tell Kennedy I need time with a potential client who might be our next big merger. It buys me the time I need. My father chooses to meet at an overly priced French restaurant next to the office. He says it helps keep our meetings more private. I think he does it to remind me that he's always close.

By the time I walk in and give the host my name, my father is already waiting. Of course he is. The small timid man walks me to a table tucked away in the back of the restaurant.

"H-here you are, sir," he says.

I take my seat. Before Thomas can dominate the conversation, I decide to start. "The merger will be official before Friday." I cross one leg over my knee.

My father scoffs. "Would've been sooner had you used Meghan like I told you to." His grubby hands grip his glass.

"Yeah, well, it's done." I cross my arms and look out into the empty dining room. "Are you drinking fucking cognac at noon?"

"What's your plan to get rid of her?" he asks, ignoring me.

"To get rid of her?" I'm not fucking getting rid of her. I'm keeping her. I just haven't figured out how yet. Not that he needs to know. He'll think I'm weak.

"Do I have to do everything?" he sneers.

"I'm not hurting her."

"She'll go to the police."

"No one will believe her. I made sure of that."

"Someone could. You need to take care of it."

"Take care of what?"

"Don't play dumb. You've handled situations like this before." He leans forward slightly.

"I'm not hurting Meghan." I do the same. I won't back down, not anymore. I'm no longer the child desperate to earn my father's love.

"I didn't say that."

"Of course you did."

The waiter arrives with his food, the silver tray shaking slightly as he sets it down.

I notice I've been offered nothing. This is no accident. Thomas Maddison is not hospitable enough to join someone in a meal. I'm the temporary intrusion on his day. The pawn he'll use to gather his information and secure his position before he tosses it away.

"Drug her. Drop her off at rehab. I don't care what you do. Just make her wildly untrustworthy, make her disappear, or make her loyal. But if it's the former, you better make sure no one ever believes her because your life fucking depends on it. If this goes wrong, it's you who will take the fall." He cuts into his food.

"I'll handle it," I say.

"Shane—"

"I said, I'll handle it." I slam a fist onto the table, and my father smiles. This is what he wanted. A reaction. He knows he has the upper hand. He's still playing a game.

"Are you still planning on coming home this weekend?" he asks eventually, between small bites.

"Wouldn't miss it." I check my watch.

"Your mother says you're bringing home a date." It's not a question.

"Yes."

"So you've finally settled down? Ready to make yourself an honest man? Rejoin the family rather than living a life on the edge of society?"

I snort. My life on the edge of society has suited him quite well. I'm not sure why he suddenly cares so much about making an honest man of me. Not when my brother has beaten me to it.

"When you find the right person, it's impossible to turn back," I say. It's true. I don't realize just how true it is until the words leave my lips.

"Ah, and here I thought it was all a play for the inheritance."

"I don't need your money, and you don't look like you're dying. And even if I did, Elise is ruthless enough to sabotage me before I even begin."

"A Maddison family trait, I'm afraid." My father flags down the waiter for the check and drops his *Amex Black* card without looking. The second it's back, he's standing and buttoning his jacket. We don't do father-son bonding, and certainly not during business hours.

As we leave, we don't shake hands. A nod of the head is all he offers me before slipping beneath an open umbrella and into the town car that waits outside. I stand and watch the taillights blur into traffic.

The walk back to the office is all the time I have to plan. My father won't let this go. I imagine the moment he's back to his office, he'll put whatever backup strategy he's had just in case into motion. That gives me an hour at most.

I have to find a way to let Meghan go without implicating the family. I won't make her relapse. I won't hurt her. Somehow, I have to convince her to keep what's happened between us. What can I offer her that she can't refuse? I already played my hand with Andrew. I suppose I could threaten to pin it on her. No, she doesn't deserve that. Killing that fucker is the least of what I could do to make up for his crimes.

There has to be a solution I'm missing. Some obvious next

steps I need to take, if only I could remain composed enough to assess and see action steps rather than emotions. I got too close, too quickly. And even though she's the one I trapped, I'm the one that can't seem to get away.

Chapter Twenty-Nine: Meghan

There's a demented anticipation with each new day. Shane hasn't tried to touch me since I told him about Andrew. I think some part of me hopes he might try again. I've started to wonder if I've scared him away, like now that he knows, he thinks I'm too broken to want. It's one of the many reasons I hate telling people. They either pity me or want to encase me in emotional bubble wrap. The thing no one gets is that both options remove my humanity. I can still want to be intimate. I can still want to be vulnerable. Or at least, I'd like to try.

Shane seemed like the type of man who wouldn't care, wouldn't think I was tainted. After all, he took what he wanted, even if that meant taking me. In some fucked up way, it made me feel safe wanting him, too.

It's not all platonic. He still kisses me, holds me, washes my hair for me whenever we shower. I can see that he still wants me. His dick always gets hard when we're together. But he never acts on it. And I'm too much of a coward to make the first move.

When he returns home early from work unexpectedly, I decide it's the perfect moment to ask him why he's been weird, but somehow, Shane beats me to the conversation.

"Would you like to leave, Meghan?" he asks.

It's not the question I was expecting, but it would explain why he hasn't tried to pressure me into sex. He doesn't want me. He's aroused by me, but by default. It's nature, not desire. He's going to let me go. I should feel excited. I should. But the wound beating in my chest doesn't cease pulsating in a hollow pain.

"You don't mean that," I say. It's easier to say that than ask why he wants to get rid of me so suddenly. After days of begging to be set free, why now? What changed?

"I swear on my life," he says.

"Well, that must be . . . nice . . . to have a life. I don't have a life to go back to, so I'm not really sure what any of this is really worth." Anger always comes out smoother than vulnerability.

"You're saying you'll stay with me then?"

"That's not what I said."

"Because if you'd rather stay . . . I can make arrangements."

"All right, fine. I'll play along. You'll let me go. What's the catch?" I fold my arms against my chest.

"You can have your freedom . . . for a price."

I roll my eyes. Of course. He's not cost me enough. "Name it."

"Be my date."

"I'm sorry?" My heart beats harder.

"Be my date for my brother's wedding this weekend."

"That's all I have to do?" I imagine putting on a dress and lipstick, dancing all night, and going home. Home-home. Surely he can't mean it. It's too easy. There has to be a catch. Maybe *wedding* is a code word, and he's really leading me to some nefarious crime headquarters where the other kidnappers gather to sell off their unsuspecting victims.

"You can't really mean it?" I challenge. The last thing I want is to be led into another arrangement without understanding all the terms.

He shrugs his shoulders. "Yes. Play the part of my loving girlfriend, help me upset my family, and I'll set you free."

"That's all I have to do?" I try to listen for the deception, or riddle, or whatever sleight of hand is happening that would cause him to offer up such an easy out.

"That's all you have to do." He takes my hand and brings it to his lips. "Be convincing, and you've earned your freedom. Do you have a deal?"

"Why am I doing this?" I eye him suspiciously.

"I hate my family. My happiness will annoy them," he says.

"And that's worth my freedom?"

"It's worth more than that." He laughs. "Do we have a deal?" He presses his lips to my knuckles.

"Deal."

The car arrives early the next morning to take us to his family's estate in the country. I'll admit, now that Mina is safely curled up in the penthouse with Ingrid, I'm less likely to consider opening a car door to jump out. I just have to pretend to be the loving girlfriend. I can do that.

I'd do anything to go home. I want to go home.

Right?

I don't know what Shane's packed for us. The people from the other night bring down four large suitcases and load them into the SUV before we leave. I watch them. I think about asking Shane if he's thought to pack me a dress and shoes for this event, but if he didn't think to do so, I don't want to be the one to remind him. For once in my life, I'm okay with the thought of being underdressed for an event. Nothing would make me happier than embarrassing him this weekend.

"Your coffee, ma'am," one of them says to me as they hold open the car door.

"Th-thank you," I say, surprised at their preparedness. I slide into the back seat and buckle in, then take a nice long sip.

"Is it to your liking, my siren?" Shane asks. He kisses the backs of my knuckles then rests his hand on my thigh.

His *Tom Ford* sunglasses are too dark to see his expression.

I hate not being able to see his eyes. It's the only way I can even begin to guess his emotions. The rest of him gives nothing away.

"It's all right," I say. I shift uncomfortably beneath his firm touch. It's innocent. Yet it makes my core clench, and my breath sticks to my lungs. This is all for my freedom, I have to remind myself. This isn't real. What I have with Shane isn't real. It's temporary. This isn't a fairytale where the dark knight turns into Prince Charming and whisks me away to a castle. Shane is my enemy. And right now, we're not on our way to a ball where we'll magically fall in love, even if he does remember my coffee order. I'm his prisoner, trapped with only one way out.

There is no happy ending for us.

CHAPTER THIRTY: SHANE

My parents aren't there to greet us when we arrive. I suppose that's to be expected. I look at my watch. It's two o'clock in the afternoon on a Thursday. Father is surely working, and god only knows how Elise fills the hours of her day.

"Welcome," I say as I open her car door and hold out my hand to help her. She shoves it aside and hops down, quick to put as much distance between us as she can. "My humble family home." I extend my arms wide in welcome. It's sarcasm, of course. There's nothing humble or family-like within this estate.

"God, Shane," she says in awe.

"That's a sweet pet name, little siren." I walk over to pull her against me and bend down to kiss her head. "A little blasphemous for the dinner table perhaps, but if you're okay with my parents knowing what we're into, who am I to judge?"

"Fuck you," she says. She tries to nudge me away with her shoulder, but I wrap my arm around her tighter.

"Oh, there will be plenty of time for that." I swoop down to kiss her neck repeatedly until I hear her reluctant giggles. The sound of her laughter warms my skin.

"I'm not fucking you," she says. It doesn't sound convincing.

"By the end of this weekend, I'll have you begging to fuck me." I wrap my arm around her waist and push us toward the front entrance.

"Not a chance."

"Oh? Care to make a wager?" I ask. I love the confidence

in her voice. I can't wait to hear it break beneath my touch.

She rolls her eyes. "There's nothing to wager. There's nothing I could want that I couldn't or haven't bought myself."

I shrug. "That's true, but that doesn't mean someone else can't buy it for you."

"I don't like gifts."

"Well, this isn't a gift." I keep a hold on her waist as I lead us through the foyer to the staircase. "This would be a prize. A hard-earned prize."

"And if you win?" She looks up at me.

"You get me a gift." I have to slow my pace with each step. It's easy to forget my legs are nearly twice as long as hers.

"What do you want?" Her eyes narrow as we reach the landing.

She's smart to mistrust me. I have expensive tastes. "What do you want?" I redirect. We pass several closed rooms. This isn't my childhood home. My parents built their estate after I graduated high school. Only my brother considers this home. I have no bedroom to return to. Instead, I take us to the primary guest suite at the end of the hall.

She doesn't respond at first. I only let go of her once we've reached the room. I open the door to allow her in first. Sunlight streams through the large bedroom windows, casting a golden glow over the room.

"A *Chanel* bag," she says, triumphant. "If I win, not only do you let me go, that's not up for debate"—she emphasizes this—"you have to buy me a *Chanel* bag. A classic bag. Small."

If she thinks I'll balk at her request, she's wrong. I'd buy her the entire fucking *Chanel* store if it made her face light up like that again. "What color?"

Her eyes widen in surprise. "Pink," she says in almost a whisper.

"Done." I unzip my hoodie and toss it on the back of the chair next to the writing desk by the windows. The bedroom is large, considering no one ever uses it. It faces the front gate. The fountain and small roundabout we parked in is visible just to the right. The room consists of a large king-size bed with an ornate gilded frame, a small writing desk, and dark wood nightstands. The floorboards are a soft brown, almost beige wood, laid in chevrons along the length of the room. A contrast to the dark burgundy and golds the rest of the space is decorated in.

"Wait, what do you want?" she asks. Her voice is a little higher than usual. I imagine she wasn't expecting me to be so agreeable. She must fear what I could want that would make me wager this. What she doesn't understand is all I want is her.

"Something from *Off-White*."

"Nothing specific?" She walks to the foot of the bed.

I shrug. "Whatever I want that day. The *Chanel* bag equivalent."

"How about I just don't turn you into the police."

I look down to find her laughing. She's joking. Her left cheek dimpled from her smile. She's teasing me. She doesn't resent me. Not yet. If I can keep my word and set her free, she could leave this weekend with a piece of her heart still open to the idea of us. I don't know what *us* could become. But I'm desperate to protect it so I can find out.

"Deal. One *Chanel* bag. Or one get-out-of-jail-free card." I hold out my hand for her to shake.

"Deal."

Chapter Thirty-One: Meghan

The butlers bring the bags to the room. Shane thanks them, shaking their hands, and smiling warmly. Watching him from the outside, I can see his appeal. He's likable. Charismatic. His physical presence demands attention and respect. Not because he's respectable, I correct myself. But because he's so tall. Tall and handsome and commanding. Yet the way he interacts with everyone allows them to feel comfortable, even welcomed by his personality. Everyone, including me.

I think I'm starting to go crazy. More than crazy. Unhinged enough to wager my life over a bag. He wants nothing from me, keeps me without demands, and agrees to my freedom in exchange for a date and make-believe. He was too agreeable, come to think of it. Too confident that he'd get me to say yes to all this. I wonder if he could really win, and if I could end up stuck with him at the end of this weekend because I begged him to fuck me and became addicted for more.

The moment the door closes, my fears are confirmed, and the real side of Shane comes out. He turns around to face me. Before I can register what he's done, he wraps me in his arms.

I resist.

He holds me tighter. I can't breathe when he traps me against him with my face pressed into his chest. Wetness pools between my legs from just this touch alone.

He's surely smearing my makeup. I turn my head so the pressure from his hug doesn't ruin my glasses along with my lipstick.

"What was that, sweetheart? I can't hear you."

I push against his stomach. "I said, I hate you."

He grabs my chin. "Say that again," he challenges. "I dare you."

"I hate you," I say and refuse to look away or even blink. He needs to understand, I mean what I say. I can't afford to feel anything else.

"Open your mouth," he says while staring down at me.

I glare up at him. *Fuck him.* I won't break or do what I'm told. It's enough that I'm his captive entertainment for the weekend. He doesn't also get to control my every move.

"Don't make me tell you twice, little siren." His thumb brushes my top lip, then pulls apart my bottom, his fingers firmly gripping my jaw. Something in my face must excite him. His brown eyes seem to sparkle at the thought.

For some reason, it makes me want to obey.

"Now, don't move. Don't close your lips." His thumb brushes against me one last time. His gaze turns black with the sadism that simmers behind them. He pauses for a moment, maybe to see if I'll move or push back, but I don't. So he leans closer and murmurs softly, "You are mine."

Then he spits in my mouth.

Shock becomes disgust as I register what he just did. I try to pull back out of his hold, but he secures me to him with a firm hand on my back while the other still cups my face.

"Swallow," he demands.

I do.

"Good girl."

I'm frozen in shock—horrified by the way my muscles clench and a pulse beats between my legs. I can't like this. It's so degrading.

"You did so well. One more time." He holds me still with one hand, and the other brushes the hair out of my face. His fingers trail across my earlobe, down the side of my neck, stopping to wrap around my throat. "Open your mouth.

Swallow. And this time, say thank you."

I don't bother responding. I open my mouth and gaze up at him, strangely excited, wanting nothing more than to close my eyes and sear those words into my memory forever.

He lowers his lips to mine and spits in my mouth. His thumb caresses my throat as I swallow. "You're so perfect." He presses his lips gently against mine as he says it. I think I'll shatter from the praise alone.

"Thank you," I say.

When he lets go of me, I stumble. My body doesn't know how to stop shaking from pleasure. I shiver. The goosebumps he's left along my back and arms are reluctant to go away, making every shift of my clothes against my skin tingle with renewed excitement.

We get ready for dinner in a comfortable silence. My mind is still recovering from the way his words made me feel. Shane slips on a pair of black trousers, fitted black t-shirt, and tightens a black leather belt around his waist. He looks every bit the bad boy I know him to be.

"What exactly is the dress code for dinner?" I ask, staring at my several unopened suitcases. I don't pack this much for vacation. I don't even know what my options are.

"Well, my parents love a show," he says as he begins to unpack for me. He lays out a simple dress. "Here, try this one," he says.

It's tea length. Casual enough to look effortless. The pale pink color will look nice against my skin. And it's brand-new, I can tell because of the tags.

Yet surprisingly, when I go to try it on, it fits.

"How did you get my size?" I ask as I emerge out of the en suite, zipping the back without a struggle.

"Ingrid is thorough. She ordered everything you'd need." He sets out a pair of shoes, as well. Everything else is put away, probably in the closets along the far side of the room.

"You bought everything new?" He went through the effort to buy me a wardrobe before I even agreed. I must be more obvious than I realize.

"Of course I did." He sounds offended.

"What if it didn't fit?"

"Then Ingrid would return it and buy you something else."

"What if it didn't look good? Would you have been embarrassed?" I give a small twirl in the mirror as I admire my silhouette. Surprisingly, it does look good. The shape is nice. Something most people wouldn't be able to accomplish for someone else. I don't know who to give the credit to, him or Ingrid. I decide on Ingrid. Shane's ego is unmanageable enough.

"Everything you wear looks good. And I would never be embarrassed by you." He kisses me gently.

I hate when he's sweet because when he is, I believe every word he says. Not just believe it. I feel it reverberate in my chest. It's as if his words sear themselves upon my soul. I can feel them on my skin and in my bones. I cling to his compliments the way someone would a cure. His praise fuels me in a way that will only leave me desperate and empty when it's gone.

I'm nervous despite myself. Even if this is pretend, I'm still meeting his family. I tell myself it's because the parents of a man like this must be even worse to have raised such a son. It's not because I want to impress them. It's not because I care.

Shane holds my hand when we walk downstairs. After this weekend, I won't see these people ever again. There's nothing to prove, no reputation to protect. This isn't my actual life. Once I leave here this weekend, I'll return to my real life. The thought should be comforting, but it isn't.

"Don't think about trying to escape." He leans over to whisper in my ear. "If you believe I'm a villain, wait until you meet my parents." He kisses the top of my head, confirming my suspicion. "I'm your safest option."

The dining room is formal. If I had any doubt about the Maddison family wealth, it disappears at the sight of a table long enough for twelve, decorated with delicate plates and cutlery beneath an elaborate crystal chandelier. As if sensing my trepidation, Shane gives my hand a squeeze and leads us toward the far end of the table, choosing the seats closest to the door, and furthest away from his family. Even in my *Burberry* dress, I feel out of place. I'm not my parents. I'm not a politician. And I'm not greedy or power-hungry enough to step on the necks of others, and these are the types of people who view that as weakness.

Wealth like this can't be built honestly. I glance from Shane's parents to him, trying to discern a difference. Shane's father is large, imposing. His shoulders take up half the width of the end of the table, his wife forced to the far edge to fit comfortably next to him. Shane looks nothing like his mother. Her blonde hair is slicked back in an elegant bun. Where his features are defined, hers are rounded. Her softness is a contradiction to the scowl on her face.

While the likeness is hard found in his mother, the opposite is true with his father. The two men look so clearly alike it's as if I'm looking into Shane's future. I wonder if their similarities are deeper than bone structure. If his father is just as ruthless as him. If that's how they afford this extravagant life.

"Father, Mother, this is Meghan. Meghan, these are my parents, Thomas and Elise," Shane says, his voice clipped. He grabs my hand beneath the table and puts it in his lap. His leg is warm against my clammy skin. I wonder if Shane can feel my nerves. "My brother, Carson, and his soon-to-be-wife, Abbey."

"It's nice to meet you, Meghan," Thomas says. He nods his head in my direction.

"Likewise," I say. It's the most I can choke out. Shane rubs his thumb back and forth against my hand. Do they know what their son has become? Do they approve? Did they make him this way? Does Shane think I'm on edge because I want to impress him?

"I see you've graduated from whores to . . ." Elise assesses me carefully, "I'll guess, assistant. No wait." She swirls her glass of wine, then points a finger at me. "Waitress. Maid?" Her eyes narrow the longer she stares. She only breaks contact to down the remaining liquid in a long series of uninterrupted gulps.

"Attorney," Shane corrects. He takes my hand from beneath the table and holds it for everyone to see. I want to flinch away beneath Elise's critical gaze, but Shane squeezes me harder. "But regardless of her chosen profession, she's mine, and I'm proud of that."

Elise looks between Shane and her husband, then back at me, some type of understanding washing over her face. It pales her cheeks in disgust.

"Oh, wonderful. You've brought your work home." She pours herself a second glass. "You're just like your father, after all." She stands, glass still in hand. Her chair scrapes loudly against the floor, filling the stunned silence, as she throws her napkin onto her plate.

I wince. I can tell it wasn't a compliment. The way everyone at the table avoids eye contact suggests outbursts like this aren't uncommon. We all stare at the place settings before us, waiting for the sound of her heels against the floor to quiet to know it's safe to resume the conversation.

Elise walks around the backside of the table, taking her time, as if to show us all that she's not embarrassed about leaving. Her long yellow dress floats behind her, like an actress in a drama, before she disappears out the door and down the hall without another word.

"Forgive Elise," his father says. He clears his throat.

"She's . . . exhausted from today's excitement. She's not herself." He offers me a tight smile before redirecting the conversation to his other son.

I want to disappear in my seat. I don't know why. I don't care about these people. This thing with Shane isn't real. But inexplicably, tears sting the corners of my eyes, and I have to blink away the onslaught of emotion before the wetness threatens to smudge my glasses and streak the makeup on my face.

"Elise doesn't matter." Shane leans over to whisper in my ear. "She's my stepmother. And my family means nothing to me." He kisses my head, then smoothes my hair with gentle strokes.

I don't want to admit her blatant disapproval bothers me. It touches a cord deep inside my frayed self-esteem. If I don't have anything to offer, I need to be likable. If I'm not likable, I'm not worthwhile. And women who aren't worthwhile are always discarded. It was true with Andrew, and it's true now. Somehow, this will end with me being used and thrown away. I've let my guard down and begun to enjoy the way Shane makes me feel. But this is a reminder that my worth is temporary, and our connection isn't real.

Chapter Thirty-Two: Shane

I can sense her unease. It rolls off of her in escalating waves. I squeeze her hand throughout dinner. I brush my thumb against her thigh in what I hope conveys comfort and reassurance. I try to catch her eye. I want to ask if she wants to leave, but at the same time, I don't want to ask a question that might upset her more. I don't know what to do to make things right.

I don't have the right. I run a hand through my hair. *Fuck.* I've never felt guilty for my work because I've never made my work my life. I've been very good at keeping the two separate. Meghan pulls at that cord of truth within me. My life and my work can never be the same now. Nothing will be the same. Even if I give her back to her life, mine will remain forever changed by her existence. She could be an ocean away, and my mind would find ways to bring her back to me. The ever-pressing need to pull the pieces of her into me is something I can't shake off.

I close my eyes. I didn't realize love could feel so much like grief.

My brother prattles on about where they've booked their honeymoon. Paris to London. So very original. Despite the way his commonness offends me, I try to listen carefully to his conversation. I fixate on his words instead of the ones inside my head, the ones telling me I've fucked everything up.

A two-week honeymoon, all booked, all pre-planned with an itinerary. The driver will pick them up from *Charles De Gaulle* and take them to the *Shangri-La*. Their room will overlook the Eiffel Tower, where they'll enjoy their first night beneath the shimmering lights of the tower. I can't feign interest after that. The blandness of their new life together is already too boring to hold my attention. I'd never take Meghan somewhere like that. We'd need to fly somewhere warm, somewhere private, somewhere she wouldn't have the need for clothes.

My dick twitches at the thought of Meghan's beautiful body, naked in the sun, relaxing at the pool of our private villa on a remote island where there's nothing to do but make her come. I adjust myself. I've done a better job at respecting her boundaries these last few days. After she told me about her assault, I knew I needed to give her the time and space to adjust. I don't want to make her submit in order to wield some false power over her sense of control. I want her to submit to me because she knows I'm the man who can unleash her pleasure.

I glance down at her to find her already looking up at me. She looks away and then back at me, as if embarrassed at getting caught. I pull her into my side. I kiss her head just so I can breathe in her scent. I love this. The way she feels. The way I feel when I'm holding her.

The tension in her shoulders relaxes the longer I hold her. Her body knows she belongs with me, even if her mind doesn't yet. I kiss her head and sweep her hair aside to kiss the back of her neck.

She moans softly, just quiet enough for me to hear alone.

Her sounds of pleasure set my nerves on fire.

I don't know how much longer I can wait. I move to straighten my shoulders and create space between us, but before I can, she grabs onto my bicep and nuzzles into me. *Fuck,* I won't make it. I can feel her nipple piercing against my arm. Her sweet green eyes look up at me while her piercing moves back and forth as she cuddles in closer.

I stroke her hair to have something polite to do with my

hands to keep me occupied.

Dinner doesn't last long. The entree is served, and dessert follows in quick succession. I don't have much of an appetite. The steak is perfectly cooked, as always, but I'm too excited for the snack I'll have in my room.

When Abbey suggests retiring early due to concerns about the final days of wedding planning, I seize the opportunity to say our goodnights and escape.

Chapter Thirty-Three: Meghan

We're only in the room a few seconds before he pulls me against his body.

"You look so fucking beautiful," he murmurs into my ear. "I've tried to give you time to accept what's happening, but I can't wait any longer." His lips brush the inner part of my lobe, then his tongue flicks over the spot.

I shiver against him. It's not just desire I feel. It's also relief. He does want me. I can feel the bulge growing against my stomach. He's been holding back, not in disgust, but in an attempt at patience. Relief floods through me. I still consider saying no or asking him why he waited so long, but the words catch in my throat as he pulls me by the arm and slams me down on the bed. Shane is not gentle. He grabs both my wrists and secures them in one of his hands. "What's our word?" he asks.

"Red," I say.

He tightens his hold.

I whimper.

He keeps me pinned against the bed as he hikes up my dress with his other hand. I'm not wearing any underwear, and he groans as he discovers me wet and waiting. "My girl is always so ready for me." He thrusts two fingers inside of me without warning and palms my clit.

It's better than anything I've ever felt. The sudden intrusion is so welcome by my body. His fingers fuck me while his thumb circles against me. The touch is lazy, yet possessive. He's in no rush to get this over with. Intimacy is different with Shane. With previous partners, any touch was obligatory or an excuse to make them come faster. Shane isn't like that. There never seems to be an endgame to his actions. As if he'd like nothing more than to do this the rest of the day.

But between his expert touch and the lust burning in his eyes, I come more quickly than I thought possible.

"Oh no, you came so easy for me. Look how sweet you are." He holds up his fingers and licks off the remaining evidence of me before shoving those same fingers in my mouth. "Do you see how good you taste?"

Any embarrassment I might have thought to feel disappears as he stares at me. His face gleams with excitement, his gaze not staying in one place too long, as if every inch of me were too beautiful to not appreciate.

"Keep sucking, just like that," he groans.

I do as I'm told. I swirl the tip of my tongue around his fingers and bite down gently as he slides his fingers out.

"Good girl. Stand so I can take off that dress," he says.

"Why?" I ask, trying to hide my excitement. The post-orgasm high doesn't sedate me like I'd like. Instead, I want more.

"Well, it's either that or risk me tearing it off you later."

"You wouldn't." A part of me hopes he will, though. It's easier when I don't have to think and don't have time to second-guess myself. I think I like being with Shane because he makes that possible.

"I would. And it would be such a shame because you look so beautiful in it."

I roll my eyes and stand. He doesn't have to stand to be able to undress me. From sitting on the edge of the bed, he can easily reach the zipper and slip it down my back.

He stares at me as he does just that.

I feel my face redden. At this angle, I can't really hide my stomach. Or the stretch marks on my thighs. I shift to move my arms to cover my body, but he stops me, grabbing my hands.

"Don't do that. Don't hide. You're so fucking perfect. Let me enjoy you."

I rub my thighs together in anticipation.

"But you didn't ask for permission before you came. And now I have to punish you." He drags me back onto bed.

"No, that's not fair," I plead. "Since when do I need permission?" I try to position myself in a way that's flattering. It's hard to relax when I'm so exposed.

"Since you became my girlfriend for the weekend." He pushes back to kneel at my feet. The mattress dips around him.

Instinctively, I wrap my arms around my middle to hide myself, but he's quick to admonish me.

"What did I say about hiding yourself?" He holds my wrists at my sides so I can't cover myself.

I groan. "You're so annoying."

"And you're a fucking goddess. I love your body. Please don't hide it. This is the last time I'll ask. Next time, I'll tie you up so you can't move." He waits to make sure I won't shy away again. Only when he looks certain does he move his touch. Slowly, he strokes up and down my legs. Then his hands grip my knees, causing my body to shake. "Ask permission this time, or I'll make it hurt."

Oh god, he's going to try to go down on me. He pushes apart my thighs before I can think to refuse. His lips and tongue caress my most intimate parts. My breath comes out in staccato gasps as an ache builds between my legs. It builds. And builds. And builds. My thighs shake. His tongue circles me as he thrusts his fingers in deep, so deep I think he'll tear me apart.

"You said you wouldn't beg," he says, pausing his assault. My hips jerk in the absence of his mouth. I'm so close.

"You don't get to come unless you beg." He bites me softly.

I squeal. He goes back to gentle strokes of his tongue. The wave that was building ebbs. *Oh no.* He said he'd bring me close to orgasm and not let me come if I was bad. I'd laughed at him at the time. I regret it now. I didn't know this kind of frustration was possible. I try to create friction against his mouth, but he holds down my thighs so I can't move.

"Ugh," I scream. The slow flick of his tongue is torture. Just when I think I can't take anymore, he eases a finger back inside of me and presses against my inner wall.

"Oh, Shane," I beg. "Please, please let me come."

A groan of approval rumbles against me as the building wave crashes into me, stealing the breath from my lungs and drowning me in an overwhelming wash of pleasure. My body shudders and clenches around him, a part of me so grateful, so awestruck, I don't regret what I've done.

He removes his fingers from inside me and brings them to his lips. "You did so well." He slides the two fingers into his mouth, making a slow show of sucking them clean. His eyes never leave mine.

I'm as stunned at his genuine desire to taste me as I am by the fact that he made me orgasm. Again. On purpose.

Shane pulls my limp body into his chest and kisses my hair. "My good girl. I'm so proud of you."

I nuzzle my head into his chest as I stare out the window.

It takes me a minute to realize I'm waiting for something. But Shane doesn't move or push me away. Instead, he strokes my hair and touches my face while sometimes interchanging the soothing attention to my back.

"Do you need anything?" he asks after a while.

"No, just this," I say. I don't know what I expected. Maybe for him to grab my face and demand I suck his dick, only for him to fall asleep when he was done and to forget about me. Definitely not this. Not him going down on me and expecting nothing in return. He doesn't even make me feel guilty for leaving him unsatisfied. He's just happy to have me in his arms.

This is what life with Shane would have been like if everything was different. But it's not. I sigh. This isn't my life. None of this is real. I'll keep my word. I have no reason to believe he'll harm me after this weekend. I begged, after all. I can agree to keep this between us.

Thunder claps in the distance. The large window overlooking the gardens is cracked, allowing the warm air to blow open our curtains as rain patters against the glass. I close my eyes. I have to leave. There's no other choice. But I can imagine what this might have felt like if he hadn't kidnapped me . . . if he hadn't ruined my life. The picture of us is so vivid. Happy. I think I could've loved him.

Of course, with what he's done, that can only be a dream.

Chapter Thirty-Four: Shane

The extended family is to arrive for dinner tonight. By noon, mostly everyone is here. My father doesn't have any living relatives. An awfully convenient contributing factor to my family's wealth.

My mother uses that as an excuse to shove her family at the forefront of importance. Her parents seem to arrive as the sun does. Grandmother Harrington prepares the cleaning staff for her expectations. Grandfather yells at the morning news. The house is spotless, but somehow the Harrington's are able to find fault.

My mother's florists arrive next, along with the bride's family. If I hoped the bride's family would make my mother more sufferable, I was mistaken. My mother and hers magnify the others' energy.

I avoid my family at all costs. Despite my original desire to annoy them with Meghan, I'm now trying to protect her from them. But dinner goes off without scandal. When we push our chairs back from the dining table, I can finally breathe a sigh of relief. We walk hand in hand to the staircase when my father stops us.

"How long will you be joining us, Meghan?" he asks.

"We're leaving after the wedding," I answer for her. I nudge the small of her back to continue forward, but my father steps into our path.

"Back to work on Monday?" he asks.

Fuck.

"Yes." I put my hand on her back and keep it there as I urge her on around him and up a step.

"And you, Meghan?" he asks pointedly.

"What?" She stops to turn to look at him.

"Are you returning to work, as well? Even after Shane gave the firm your rehab records?"

"I'm sorry?" She sidesteps my touch. Her jaw drops at the claim.

"Oh . . . I assumed he told you. He destroyed your career, after all."

She looks at me, and then my father, and back again. Then she walks up the stairs without another word. Deadly calm.

"Fuck you," I say to my father and then go after her.

I walk into the room, nervous for the first time I can remember. I didn't want her to find out like this. I wanted to tell her on my own time, in my own way. To explain myself. Now I'm forced to defend.

"You told them I went to rehab?" Her jaw hangs open in surprise. Worse than surprise. In fear. Whatever else she wants to say is unable to come out. After all the things I've put her through, done to her, never once has she looked at me like a threat.

"I did what I had to do to discredit you." I start to gently explain. I don't want to scare her. I'd never hurt her. Not even like this.

"For what gain? Or was your plan always to destroy my life." Her lips tremble. I wish she would scream at me. Hit me. Anything except cry. I don't like these tears. I don't want to cause her real pain. I told her I'd never leave her empty, and I meant it. Or I wanted to.

"I didn't want to destroy your life, Meghan." I step toward her, but she steps away. I sigh. I keep my distance as I talk. "I wanted to ensure the merger would go through. To keep you from finding things that might cause you to sway your client into backing out."

"Kennedy will just find it. You've replaced me only to have someone else finish the job."

I shake my head. "Kennedy didn't find it. It's done." I know my words have hurt her. But I know the words that come next will hurt her even more. "They were never going to make you partner. Here," I say, handing over my phone with the pictures of the file my father's men gathered. "You don't have to believe me. See for yourself."

Her hands tremble as she takes it from me. She sits down on the bed and scrolls through what I know will gut her to the core. With each flick of her finger, the emotion sets in more. I can see it in the lines of concern that furrow her brow and in the way her lips set into a thinning line.

"I don't want to see this. Get out. Get out," she whispers. "I don't want to be near you," she says, stronger. She throws the phone across the room.

"Meghan," I say. I need her to understand I had no choice, but I still managed to choose her. She needs to read everything to understand. I need her to understand so we can move forward.

"I want to go home, or I want you to get out."

"There's nowhere for me to go," I start.

She snorts. "I don't fucking care."

"Meghan, let me explain—"

"I think you've explained enough." She throws a blanket and a pillow to the ground. "I fully understand who you are now, Shane. I don't need to know you any more, thank you."

I want to fight back, but there's no fight left in her. I can see it. It makes me want to burn everything to the ground.

I take my pillow and lie in front of the door. It's important for her to know she can't get rid of me, even when she's mad, even when she doesn't choose me. I will always choose her.

We spend the night apart.

I wonder if I've pushed her too far.

Chapter Thirty-Five: Meghan

Shane sleeps on the floor. A part of me expected him to fight back, to climb into bed with me and hold me against him until the anger faded. But he never does. I don't know whether to find comfort or disappointment in the empty space next to me. It's the first time he's listened to me say *no*.

I dress for breakfast without speaking. He must lie awake, waiting for me, because the second I slip on a dress, he's standing next to me, ready to go.

Breakfast is tense. No one speaks, and the meal is overly formal. There's no warm family gathering. It's a full-seated meal. Elise hasn't returned, which is a letdown. I was eager to have someone else to take this frustration out on.

I don't eat my eggs. I drink my coffee and decide I'll never forgive him. I knew this was too good to be true. He's not just ruined my career. He's used my lowest moments against me. He leveraged my suffering for his goals. I can never be with a man like that.

I wonder who'll break the silent treatment first. My bet is him. I could thrive off this anger for months. He's the one who can't keep his eyes off of me.

I'm done eating, and I push back from the table. I don't wait for anyone else or offer an explanation. I round the corner when Shane catches up to me. He grabs my wrist and whirls me around to face him.

"Cut the theatrics, Meghan. You'll forgive me eventually, anyway. Tell me what it'll take for us to skip all this and go right to what I can do to make you feel better."

"You can never fix what you've done." I pull away.

He rolls his eyes. "You've already forgiven me. You just don't want to admit it to yourself."

"That doesn't even make sense." I walk past him and head up the stairs, taking it two at a time. I just need to get away from him.

I can hear his footsteps close behind.

"Of course it does. That's how you are. You want things you tell yourself are wrong, so you suppress the desires. I don't just mean with me. It's everything. You allow yourself to be held hostage by some narrative society has told you is appropriate, and now you refuse to deviate. You hate your career, your friends, even your life. Yet you continued on. Doing the same things that planted your misery, somehow hoping happiness might grow. The path society created for you will never make you happy, Meghan. I did you a favor."

"Tell yourself whatever you need to feel better," I say dismissively. I walk into our room with every intention of slamming the door in his face, but he catches it. "You don't need to lie to me at this point. The weekend is almost over. You won the bet. I'll keep my promise. Let's just avoid each other as much as we can the rest of our time together."

"Meghan, stop. Listen to me. You need to hear this. They were never going to make you partner."

"You can't know that," I scream. It feels so good to let it out. "You can't know that, Shane. You know nothing about me."

"Look for yourself. Actually look." He hands me his phone again, open to the screenshots of the managing partners' emails. My eyes scan left to right. This time, I take in every word. It was never going to be me. Jeremy and Sophia are making partner. After all those years. Everything I worked for, all the long nights, the sacrifices I made, the plans I'd canceled in order to work more. The relationships I lost. All of it was for nothing.

I have nothing to show for my dedication besides the title next to my name.

"They were never going to make you partner," he says softer. "I'd say I'm sorry, but I'm not. You deserve better than just Morgan & Miller. You're not just another lawyer. You deserve to be and have whatever you want. You're so smart, Meghan. You're more than just your career. You get to be whoever you want to be, not who everyone expects you to shape yourself after."

His words set in like a weight dropped in my stomach. Every day of my life seemed to be building to the moment I would stand in front of my parents and my peers and proudly proclaim that I'd made it. That my career status was my finish line, and I'd crossed over into success. I wagered my entire twenties on the belief that a career would be the thing that made me complete, only to find the pieces of me more shattered than when I began.

I don't recognize who I've become or who I was. I don't know who Meghan is without the firm. I don't know what my value is without my career.

The words start to blur as nausea crawls up my skin. I can't look at my rejection any longer. I close out his photos, wishing to smash his phone against the ground but ready to hand it back when the familiarity of his home screen catches my attention. It's me. I bring the screen closer to my face. His wallpaper is me, my face, my face after an orgasm, one he must have taken the other day.

"Why is this your home screen?" I hold up his phone as evidence.

"It's your orgasm face," he says with a smirk. He looks from the phone back to me.

"I know what it is. I remember you taking the picture. But why is it your background?"

"It's not obscene. No one knows. No one but me." His smirk becomes a full-blown grin.

"Shane," I groan. He's right. It's not obscene. But that's not what bothers me. "I look awful. This is what you want to see? I'm a mess." My eyes look half open in bleary ecstasy. My skin is bare. Any imperfection is visible, since he took the picture so close.

"Yes. But you're gorgeous. Even more gorgeous because I made a mess of you. It's my favorite picture."

"It's your only picture of me." I roll my eyes.

"Something I'd like to change."

This is too much. It's like the room is closing in around me. Heat starts to overwhelm my body. It starts at my neck and creeps down my skin. Suffocating me.

I can't keep up playing pretend. It makes it hurt worse. I already mourn what could have been. And now I'm fantasizing about being his. Maybe it's the orgasms or the dresses and the gifts, but all of this combined makes me break.

"I can't do this anymore," I say, choking.

"Meghan, we talked about this, don't be ridiculous." He takes back his phone and slips it into his back pocket.

"It's not that." I shake my head.

"What is it then?" he asks.

"I can't pretend anymore. It hurts too much. It makes me want it. And I can't want this, Shane." The only thing worse than my failed career are the remnants of my broken relationships. Shane is just another name to add to a long list of heartbreak. Just additional proof that nothing lasts because I'm so fucked up that self-destruction is the only tendency that comes easily.

"Why can't you want this?"

"Because none of it is real! You kidnapped me. You're making me your whore in exchange for my freedom. You've ruined my life. We can't just pretend like this'll work."

"We can do whatever the fuck we want." He sounds mad.

"It'll never work. Maybe I can forgive you, I don't know. But I'll never forget. And we'll never be the same."

Chapter Thirty-Six: Shane

I grab her face and squeeze until I see the pain turn to excitement in her eyes. "Are you not listening? I'm not discarding you. I'm making my claim."

"I don't know what that even means, Shane!" she yells. The tears that fall now aren't sad. They're angry. The emotion I love so much falling freely.

"It means whatever you want it to. Kidnapper. Boyfriend. Partner. I don't care what you call it. But you're mine. I'm not leaving. And the world will know it once we leave this room. It doesn't have to be for pretend."

"So I get to become your pet while you, what, Shane? While you get to live your life and fuck whoever you want, doing whatever you want? No thank you. I decline. I don't want what you have to offer. I might be a failure, but I refuse to allow myself to become someone who relies on another just to simply exist."

"Do you want me to fuck other people?" I ask.

She looks startled by the honesty and directness of the question.

"W-what?" she asks.

"Do you want me to fuck other people?" I say again.

She doesn't answer.

"Answer me." I squeeze harder. I can feel her teeth beneath her skin, see her pulse quicken in that beautiful neck. "When I let you go, do you want this to end? Do you want me to fuck other people?"

"No," she cries harder.

A strange twinge of pride swells in my chest. I've never found monogamy compelling. Not the idea of one woman. Contrary to what she believes, I don't view women as objects to be used sexually. It's more the notion that one person could or should fulfill all needs. It seems to guarantee failure. Disappointment. Resentment. But with Meghan, I want things I never imagined I would feel. I want to own her. Dominate her. Submit to her. In all ways imaginable. She won't have a need for anyone else because no one else could provide to her what I can. What I will.

I mean what I said that Meghan is my siren. Since the day I met her, I've been unable to get her out of my mind. I think of her, hear her sweet voice in my mind when she's not even there, smell her jasmine perfume long after she's left a room, and I dream of her soft body struggling against the power of mine.

Monogamy isn't a concept I understood. Now it's not enough. If there was a way to get closer to her, deeper inside of her, consume her more to keep her forever, maybe then I would feel satisfied.

Until then, I'll settle for this.

"I won't be yours," she says. "I can't be, not after all you've done. But I don't want you to be someone else's. I don't know what that means. Maybe you can have my body, but I don't think I can ever give you my heart."

"It's a start." I smile, and her eyes narrow. I have her desire, and I'll earn her trust. Our relationship has been building to this point for days. She knows what's coming, and I can't wait any longer. I slip my hands beneath her dress and run my hands over her stomach.

I ease the fabric over her and start to worship her body.

"No," she says. "This isn't what I meant."

"No?"

"No."

"I'm not going to stop unless you say *red*, Meghan," I say.

"I'll still fight back," she whispers. She licks her lips.

I push her back onto the bed. "I hope you do. It'll just make me harder."

She gapes at me. Maybe she thought I was lying before. She can fight back all she wants. It's only giving me more satisfaction.

"I'll escape," she says, regaining that defiance I adore. But her movements say otherwise. She scoots back onto the bed, not to escape me like she claims, but to create space for me to crawl on top.

"And I'll chase you down and tie you up tighter." I take my shirt off and climb onto the bed after her.

"You're fucked up, getting off on all this."

"Am I? Tell me, if I were to slip my hand between your thighs, what would I find? Hmm? Would I find your body unwilling?" I trail my fingers against her leg.

"I don't want you," she says. But even she doesn't believe those words. Her thighs tremble. Her chest heaves.

"Your body says differently."

"It's a reaction. I can't control it."

"No, you can't. But I sure can." And I push apart her thighs with one knee.

She struggles against me.

"You're mine, and you know it. You want whatever I need."

Chapter Thirty-Seven: Meghan

I've fantasized about this exact moment for what feels like my entire life. This is what sex was always meant to be. This is how it was portrayed in my books and on the screen. But the sex I've had has never felt intimate, only performative. I played an actor in a scene of my life that only needed to end in his satisfaction, never my own. The *his* wasn't important. It could be anyone. They were all the same. They all fucked the same. I don't think I could even articulate what would make me feel adored before Shane. I don't think I knew simple touches could feel so powerful or kisses could feel so intimate. But with every touch, time slows. And with every kiss, I feel myself responding to raw pleasure instead of forced joy.

"I'm not yours," I say. I don't believe that anymore. Something about this week with Shane has shifted the emotions in me for good.

"This is mine. This pussy is mine. That face. Those tears. Everything about you belongs to me."

I spit in his face.

He just smiles wider, the sick fuck. He wipes it away with his thumb and forces apart my mouth, making me suck it off of him.

"Every time you defy me, you add a punishment."

I have a moment of realization. I'm not going to escape him this time. He's going to take me. And as much as I wish I could deny him, a part of me hopes he means what he says, that he'll really take what he wants. And a growing part of me hopes he'll never give me back.

"Are you going to hurt me?" My voice sounds quiet. Fragile. I'm on the verge of breaking, not out of fear, but nerves. Will sex with Shane feel as good as everything else does with him?

"Would you get off on it if I do?" He watches my face.

I consider lying. I want to. I don't want to give him that satisfaction yet. What I should want is to spit in his face again and roll away, running and screaming until someone comes to my rescue and saves me from this man. Prince Charming might not exist, but villains clearly do. Yet, as I stare into those dark eyes, I see the lust I secretly feel reflected back at me, and that growing piece of me gives in. I can't hide it anymore.

"I think so," I admit.

It's the permission he's waited for.

"Don't take your eyes off mine." He moves off of me only to take off his boxers, a part of his leg still touching mine, as if not trusting me to stay put.

I don't do as I'm told. I can't take my eyes off his dick.

Shane moves on top of me. Hovering just above my body so as not to put all his weight on me. There's no way it's going to fit.

His hand moves from my throat to my face. His fingers squeeze my jaw as he moves my face to see me better. "I said, look at me."

Shane eases himself between my legs. My heart hammers in my chest. He places the tip of his dick on my clit, moving it back and forth, slowly, torturing me, making my stomach clench as the swelling sensation builds within me.

"You look away, and I stop," he warns.

I feel my bottom lip tremble. I do my best to obey, but it's impossible. The sensation of him against me, almost where I want him, is torture.

He moves his dick to my entrance, then back again to my clit, in a slow-building rhythm that causes my hips to move involuntarily, desperate to increase the friction.

"You're so wet for me," he says on a groan.

A small whimper escapes my lips. I can't take it anymore. I'm about to give in and beg him to fuck me. With each tease of his dick, my sanity comes undone. I close my eyes as he circles me again, increasing the pressure steadily until my back arches and I press my chest into his.

Shane groans in approval. "You're so ready for me." He lowers his body down to mine, propping himself up on the elbow he's trapped my head next to. He stills himself at my entrance as he kisses my forehead softly, my face still in his hands, as the tip of his dick slips inside.

It should hurt. It always hurts. Not from the kink. No one before Shane tried anything quite as aggressive, nothing that could actually cause the type of pain I secretly wanted. But it would hurt. Like dry sandpaper. I'd cling to their shoulders and pray the end to come quick. With Shane, there's no pain. And there should be. His dick is bigger than any I've ever seen. Thick and hard and surely too long to fit inside of me. But he pushes in, filling me fuller than I thought possible in a way that's more satisfying than anything I've ever felt.

The pain only comes after. When his hand returns to my throat, as he chokes me until my head swarms with pleasure, and he whispers in my ear, "You're taking me so well, Meghan."

I can't help but moan in relief. He thinks I'm good. It makes my heart beat faster.

"You feel how wet you are for me?" He thrusts harder. He moans. "Your pussy knows it's mine."

There's something so intimate about missionary that I never experienced before Shane. His eyes don't leave mine. Not once. It's like claiming my body isn't enough, and he's reaching for my soul.

I come. He swallows my breath, taking in every piece of

my pleasure. He kisses his way down my jaw to the base of my neck.

"Meghan." He moans as he rests his forehead against mine while he pushes himself into me one last time. "Oh, god, Meghan."

He stills. Our breathing syncs. We hold on to each other.

"God, you feel so good. You did so well, little siren." He kisses me as he eases himself out of me. "It's like you were made for me."

I move to roll out of bed and clean myself up, but he stops me.

"No, don't. I can do that. Let me take care of you."

He doesn't bother putting on clothes. He reaches down to grab his discarded shirt and uses it to wipe away the cum that covers my thighs.

"You came inside me." I state the obvious. I'm still too stunned at how good it felt to feel anything else.

"I did." He wipes the other thigh. Then he takes his fingers and pushes the remaining cum back inside of me. "I like the idea of filling you with my cum." He pumps his fingers twice more before slipping them out.

"You didn't use a condom," I say.

"I'm clean. I test before and after every partner." He licks us off of his fingers.

"Aren't you concerned about me?"

"Not really."

"Shane . . ." He doesn't strike me as irresponsible. I don't like his rash decisions. He could regret this. He could regret me. And then I would truly have nothing.

"Modern medicine is a miracle." He stands up.

"Shane!"

"What? I want you. I made that decision. That's what matters." He turns his back to leave the bedroom and head into the bathroom.

"What if I get pregnant?" I call after him.

"Are you on birth control?"

"Yes, but—"

"Do you want me to get you the morning-after pill? Would it make you more comfortable? I can do it right now." He walks back into the room.

"No, it's not that," I say.

He sighs, then walks over to me and pulls me out of the bed. "No more worries. Let me take care of you. Would you like me to start you a bath?" He kisses the top of my head.

I groan. "I would." I try to take a blanket with me and wrap it around my body, but Shane catches me and takes it away, tossing it back onto the bed as he walks me to the bath.

"Give me a second," I say. I push against his chest. I need a moment alone to pee.

"I want to take care of you, Meghan," he begins.

"I know, I know." I push him away again. "And I'll let you, I promise. I will. But I get to use the bathroom alone, okay?"

"Okay." He grins when he realizes I'll comply.

He's patiently leaning against the door frame when I open it. I can't help but roll my eyes at his enthusiasm.

Shane helps me into the bath. He doesn't let me do a thing. He never does. All I can do is relax in the warm water. He washes my hair for me. He washes my body. He kisses me. When I'm done, he even insists on drying me off.

I could get used to this.

"Come, let me hold you, my little siren," he says after gently towel-drying my hair.

I follow behind him, eager to get beneath the warmth of the duvet.

"Why do you call me that?" I ask. We lay tangled together.

"What? My little siren?"

"Yeah." I readjust myself in his arms so I can see his face.

He doesn't answer right away. His fingers stroke my hair.

I nudge him with my shoulder.

"Isn't it obvious?"

"Not to me."

"I've told you before."

"So tell me again. I like to listen."

He chuckles. "Have you ever read the *Odyssey*?"

I resist my instinct to be a smart ass since he's opening up. "Of course I've read the *Odyssey*."

"Well, you're my siren."

"I'm your destruction?" I can't keep the hurt from my voice.

"No." He pauses. "Yes." He squeezes me. "You are my weakness. It's inexplicable. It's more than how you look or sound or the things you do. It's magnetic. In the best and worst of ways, you call to me. Even when you're not there. Since the day I met you, you're like a presence I can't separate from. Just the thought of you creates a longing that pulls me back, no matter what it costs me."

It sounds like it makes him sad. My heart aches. Maybe he doesn't want this either. Maybe we're both trapped by whatever this pull is between us, neither of us able to escape.

Chapter Thirty-Eight: Shane

Sex with Meghan is better than I imagined, and I imagined it a lot. We spend the rest of the afternoon having sex and holding onto one another. I have lunch brought to the room so we don't have to get dressed. I never want her to wear clothes again. I hate knowing I have to leave her tonight, even if it's only for a few hours.

"I won't be long. It's a formality," I explain. I lean down to kiss her head.

"It's your brother's bachelor party." She rolls her eyes.

"Exactly." I grin.

"What are you guys gonna do?"

"Probably sit around drinking scotch, talking about who has the bigger dick and the most money."

"Sounds exciting."

I lean down to kiss her head. "It's less exciting when you always win. I'll be back soon. If you're good while I'm gone, I'll let you come again."

Her blush is the last thing I see as I close the door.

The Maddison Men bachelor party. I opt for one of the worn leather chairs tucked away in the corner. I slouch across it. My legs are too long to sit comfortably.

I'm sure this isn't my brother's actual bachelor party, in the lounge in our parent's home. I don't pretend to care. Carson and I have never been close. I'm seven years older. The mistake. He's the protege. The golden boy. The Harvard grad who's about to marry his college sweetheart. A woman from good middle-class parenting. Wholesome. A future *Good Housekeeping* cover model. The type of woman Elise probably expects us both to marry in order to create another standard in which I'm guaranteed to fail. A woman like Abbey would never love someone like me. It's not tragic. The feeling is mutual. I have no use for the perfect American wife. A balanced career woman, mother, and doting partner. That's how I always thought of marriage, which is probably why I dismissed the concept. Such an arrangement would never be comfortable for me.

Luke, one of the groomsmen, hands out the cigars.

"To Carson's last day of freedom," Marc says. He holds up his glass in salute. The others follow suit.

How cliché. I don't raise mine. It's idiotic to correlate marital status with freedom. If Carson really thinks marrying Abbey equates to a loss of manhood, then he's dumber than he looks for going through with it. It's a gutless move to agree to monogamy and then blame the woman. Men are just as complicit in passionless relationships.

Probably more so.

"Do me a favor. Wait until after the first year to start popping out children. It changes everything," Nate says.

It takes everything not to stand up and leave. How boring and predictable. A bachelor party that complains about the very institution they've all willingly agreed to. I take a sip of my drink and watch the clock. I hate wasting my time. Especially when it could be better used finding ways to make Meghan scream my name.

"A little too late for that," Brett laughs. He clasps Carson on the shoulder.

My brother looks uncomfortable. The mood shifts. Each of the groomsmen stare into their glasses of liquor as if hoping to drown inside them.

"Goddamnit, Brett," Carson says.

"No, go ahead, son, continue," my father says calmly, eyeing Brett with disdain. My father might not like family secrets being kept from him, but he hates disloyalty even more. A friend who can't keep a secret is nothing more than an enemy that's allowed to sit too close.

"We didn't want to say anything until she was further along. It's still too early to start telling people. But Abbey's pregnant." Carson takes a long drink and pours himself another.

I consider my brother. If he's happy, I'll be happy for him. The idea of having kids in this world seems borderline masochistic, but I'll try not to judge. Just a few hours ago, Meghan worried about the same thing. For the first time in my life, I understood how someone might hope for a different outcome.

Maybe love does make a person lose their mind.

"Better be sure it's yours," Luke says and laughs. "She did pressure you into a quicker wedding. Maybe she's trying to trap you."

Marc hits him in the chest before telling him to shut up.

"The boy's right," my father says. "You need to be sure."

I grind my jaw. His cool, calm words set my nerves on edge. He would fucking know.

"I'm sure, I'm sure." Carson takes a long drink and sets it down with a clink against the tabletop. "I have a guarantee it's mine." He takes another drink and grins. All irritation slips away from his face as he looks around the room. Pride radiates off of him.

"You can never be certain," my father starts.

"Abbey was a virgin?" Luke interrupts. He wiggles his eyebrows.

"God, what the fuck is your problem?" Marc hits him again.

Carson runs a hand through his hair. It's the only time I see a resemblance in us. Our dark hair is the only trait we have in common.

"Yeah, well, like I said, I'm certain."

"That's how it should be done," Luke says as Marc takes his drink away from him. "I'm only gonna marry a virgin. I don't want all the hassle." He says this matter-of-factly, as if it's common sense. As if it's such a mundane observation that we'd all agree.

I grip my glass. I never understood virgin kinks—it's fucking weird. But, of course, Luke only wants to marry a virgin. The only reason a grown man worries about anyone's sexual history is if they're someone like Luke. Limp dick. No clue how to make someone come. It's probably less embarrassing with someone who doesn't know any better. I take another small sip of my drink. I'm not insecure or incompetent, so I've never felt the need to be anyone's first.

I think of Meghan. I don't love the thought of another man with her. Clearly, I'm willing to kill any man that's hurt her. But who she is and what she's done before me has only made her the woman she is today. The beautiful, feisty, passionate woman. Unafraid of anything or anyone but me. I smile to myself. I don't understand wanting someone only because they're a virgin. But I'm starting to understand wanting to be someone's last.

"Does she get the ring?" Marc asks, his eyes shift to my father.

Another uncomfortable energy shift sweeps over the room. Carson repositions himself in his chair. He recrosses his legs and finishes his second glass. The other groomsmen look at the floor.

My father doesn't even blink. I don't think I've ever seen the man uncomfortable in my entire life. I forgot about that ring. The Maddison family heirloom. A two-carat emerald-cut diamond passed down to the first married son of the family. But my father clearly doesn't think Abbey is worthy of that ring.

The ring belonged to Thomas's mother. I never met my grandmother. She died a few days before I was born. She gave the ring to him in hopes that he'd one day give it to the love of his life. But father could never marry her, so he gave the ring to no one.

I wonder what he's playing at, keeping the ring to himself. I'm not naive enough to think he's kept it for me, the bastard son. He never thought I'd marry. I'm not the one to inherit the family business.

Once everyone is fully drunk, the guys talk about what they want to do next and decide on going out. But drunk men are hard to corral, so Carson does his best to get them to decide on a bar. My father uses that as his sign to leave for the night. I give it another minute. The last thing I need is to end up trapped alone with my father. When I'm sure he's been gone long enough to retire to his bedroom, or dungeon cellar, or wherever he spends his evenings, I take my leave, as well.

Chapter Thirty-Nine: Meghan

I grow tired of waiting for Shane. I have too much energy. I walk around the mansion. It seems a strange concept to get lost in a person's home. But I've done just that. I find a long hallway I haven't seen before. A faint light emanates from a cracked door.

"Meghan?" A voice calls after me.

Shit. He saw me.

"Meghan," Thomas says again. "Why don't you come in?"

Shit, shit, shit. I take a deep breath and open the door.

Thomas sits in a large leather armchair with a glass of whiskey in his hand. His button-down shirt is unbuttoned at the top. His suit jacket is hanging off the back of the chair. The fireplace simmers behind. Its dying embers cast a soft glow across the scene. The parts of the room its light can't reach are obscured in an eerie shadow.

I thought he'd be at the bachelor party. I thought everyone would be gone.

"Sit." It's not a question. And he's not Shane. I don't feel like testing his boundaries. "Meghan. You're a bright woman," he says.

"Thank you," I say, uncertain where he's going with this.

"My son seems quite fond of you." He swirls his glass and watches the amber liquid settle.

Oh good. My shoulders relax a little. I'm a great actor. "We're quite fond of each other," I say. It's not completely a lie. I think of today, and my cheeks heat.

"I'm sure you are."

I don't like how he said it. I try not to fidget in my seat as I wait for him to speak again. I don't want to say the wrong thing and reveal all my cards.

"I believe we'll be better off as allies, so let's not lie to each other."

"Okay . . ."

"You have a deal with my son." Another statement.

"Why do you care?" There's no use denying it. He clearly didn't call me in here because he was missing a piece of information.

"I'd like to make my own deal," he says. He takes a drink. "Since you can stand to be in my son's company longer than any person he's brought home before, let's join forces and turn the tables on him."

"How would I do that?" I shove my hands beneath my thighs to keep myself from revealing my unease.

"Marry my son."

"I'm sorry?" I feel as if I might throw up. The dark edges of the room start to creep closer. I heard him wrong.

"Marry Shane."

"I can't . . . I can't just marry him. Even if I wanted to, he'd also have to be willing." And I definitely don't want to marry him.

"Let me worry about that. Shane isn't the only one who can make a power move. We'll announce your engagement at dinner tomorrow night. Take back the upper hand."

"Why would I tie myself to him for life when he says he'll let me go at the end of this weekend? What could you possibly offer me that would make me choose to stay?"

He laughs deeply. "Do you really think my son will let you go? After all this?"

"He said he would." My words come out more quietly than I intend. I think of his lips against my skin. The way it felt to be pressed against him. Could the passion behind his touch translate to something more?

It makes him laugh harder. "Shane won't keep his word. I know my son better than he realizes. He'll never let you go. Your best chance at a normal life is to align yourself with someone more powerful. Or become someone more powerful. I can help you do both. Take my offer."

"What do I get in return?" I ask hesitantly. I don't know if I can trust Shane, but I definitely can't trust his father.

"A career, the thing you've always wanted. Marry my son, and I'll make you partner at my law firm. Hell, marry my son, and one day you'll be the managing partner of the firm. You have no career to go back to now."

I shake my head. "That's not enough. I could go back, explain myself. They'll believe me."

He no longer laughs. He sets his glass down with force. "You have nothing to go back to, my dear."

"I could, I could go back. I don't want my career given to me. I'm not like you. I want to earn what I have."

"Take my offer or have nothing."

"No." I shake my head. "I'll go back and explain myself, and they'll—"

"You have nothing to go back to. I made sure of it."

"Y-you?" My mind races. Shane did this. Shane ruined my life, my career. And when that wasn't enough, he ruined sex for me with anyone else.

"You think my son would have used your sobriety against you? The boy doesn't have the grit." He laughs.

The surprise doesn't weigh heavy for long. My thoughts start churning. I was so hard on him, and he took it. He took it. He treated me with care. Even when faced with the impossible, he still found a way to choose me.

I shake my head. "Why ruin me only to offer me a lifeline?"

"Because I like my people to have loyalty. And rock bottom ensures the ultimate loyalty."

"I'll just divorce him," I say. I know the words hold little sway as soon as they leave my lips. I'm not even sure they're true.

"Fine. Sign the agreement. Stay married one year, and I'll make you partner, and I'll provide the support you'll need to get away from Shane once it's over."

"I wanted to earn my career," I start to say, more to myself than to him. I never wanted to become my parents. I didn't want to become someone who relied on others for their success. I wanted to become my own person. I wanted to become successful on my own. I wanted to make a difference.

"An idealist. I pity you." He takes another sip of his drink. "But I admire you. No one earns everything they have, my dear. Take my deal. Run my law firm. Use it as penance for whatever grave moral sin you feel you're committing in leveraging this opportunity. I knew you would be the right person all along, and truly, you've proved it."

"You planned all this." The pieces start to click together.

His fingers form a steeple as he peers at me from over his hands. "Perhaps."

"Why?" I ask.

"You don't need to know why," he says.

"That's not fair."

"I'm not in the game of fairness, my dear. Take my deal." He pushes the papers forward on the table. Like he always knew we would meet here. "I'm offering you a way out. Money, prestige, security. All I need in return is for you to continue what you're doing. Pretend to be a happy couple. Except this time, you have an ally instead of a prison."

I take the contract to read.

"You have until I finish this glass to sign. If you've not agreed by then, the deal is void."

He picks back up his half-empty glass. I watch him for only a second, then sign against my better judgment. He takes back the papers and slides them into the inner pocket of his jacket as he takes out a box. He slides the small velvet square in exchange.

"Congratulations," he deadpans.

I take the box. It shakes as I open the lid, revealing a beautiful emerald-cut diamond.

"I always wanted a daughter-in-law ruthless enough to deserve the family name." He stands to leave. "I know you won't disappoint me." His hand clasps my shoulder for a brief second. Then he walks out the door.

I slide the ring on my finger and groan. It fits perfectly. It's elegant, extravagant, but somehow perfect. Everything I didn't know I wanted. Like this stupid man. I take the ring off, shove it back in its box, and bury it deep within my pocket.

How will I hide this from Shane? Regret turns to outrage. I don't need to feel bad for Shane, the man who ruined my career, kidnapped me, and kept secrets. This is exactly what he deserves. And using him in marriage is no worse than all the things he's done to me.

I get back to the room, relieved to have the time to process alone. When I hear the door unlock, I hide the ring in my suitcase.

"W-what are you doing back so soon? Shouldn't you still be at the party?" I ask Shane as he walks in the door.

"Didn't feel like staying," he says. He shoves his hands in his pockets as he leans against the doorway. "What are you doing?" He sounds suspicious. He knows something is wrong.

"I need to go workout," I say. A truth. "Did you pack me any running clothes?"

"No," he says. "I didn't think you'd need the additional exercise." He smiles. He's always smiling at me.

"Well, do you have anything? I need to do something. I

can't just sit here." I throw my hands in the air. His charm is only going to irritate me more. I need to get away from him or guilt will set in.

Shane watches me. Confused, probably. Of course he doesn't understand my frustration. How could he? And I'm not gonna be the one to explain it. This is his father's scheme. He can be the one to tell him.

"I have sweatpants. And a t-shirt I can give you. Will that work?" Shane offers eventually.

"Give them to me," I say.

"I don't have any sneakers. At least none that will fit you." He pushes off the doorframe and walks over to his side of the dresser.

"I'll figure it out," I snap.

"There's a gym downstairs. You can lift weights." His tone is still kind even as my agitation shows.

"Perfect." I grab the *Vans* from my stuff. "Fuck, I don't have any music." The dick still has my phone, and the temporary one he gave me doesn't connect to the internet, so there's no music.

"Here, use mine." He tosses his phone to me, then his headphones. "Give me yours. In case you need to text me," he adds.

"You'll let me use your phone? Unsupervised?" I hold it as if it might decide to burst into flames at any moment.

He shrugs his shoulders. "If you wanted to call for help, you would've found a way by now."

He's right. I run my fingers through my hair. I haven't even tried to leave him. I can't afford to stop and question why that's true. I need to stop thinking. I need to work out.

"Are you okay?" he asks. He takes a tentative step toward me.

"I'm fine."

"You know, you could tell me if —"

"I said I'm fine."

He shifts uncomfortably. I don't think I've ever seen Shane uncomfortable. The guilt pulses between us. He shoves his hands into his pockets.

"It's in the basement. Down the hall, past the living room. The third door on the left. Text me if you need anything."

Chapter Forty: Shane

Something's wrong. I can't let it go. I won't let her shut me out again. Not after today. We've made too much progress to ruin it now.

I sneak downstairs to see her. The weight of the conversation with the other men weighs on me. I don't want to be her Luke. A man who traps a woman into loving him. She deserves better than that. But I'm not too much better. So I'll offer her an out.

If she wants her freedom so badly, she can earn it. I'll give her a head start. If she can run and make it to the road before I catch her, I'll let her go. No more games. I'll have Beth drive her home tonight.

But if I catch her, she's mine to keep.

I find her lifting weights in the gym. I love seeing her in my clothes. I want her to always have a piece of me. My heart aches at the thought that this could go wrong. That I could lose her. But I won't keep her any longer.

I must scare her because she jolts as I remove an *AirPod* from her ear.

"The deal is off," I say the words before I can lose my nerve.

"W-what?" she asks.

"The deal is off." It's easier to get the words out the second time.

"What? Why?" She slips the headphones back into their case. Her fingers shake.

"I don't want to pretend anymore," I say.

"What are you—"

"New game. If you outrun me, I'll let you go."

"Shane . . ." She looks up at me with big, bright eyes.

"Make it to the road, on the other side of the creek, in front of the house, and I'll let you go tonight. No conditions." I'm still in my jeans and button-down. She should have the advantage like this. Even if it's minimal. It's important that I don't have the upper hand this time.

"Shane, what are you —"

"I'll give you a ten-second head start."

"Shane."

"Nine." It'll take her at least a minute, maybe two, to find her way outside. There's a chance I could have her before she even breaks the door.

"You can't be serious." She bites her lip.

"Eight."

She takes off. I watch her disappear around the corner. I hear her little feet frantically climbing the stairs. I keep my word. I count down to zero before taking off. The house is quiet except for our footsteps. Hers are still staccato. My little prey is desperate for escape.

I'm surprised she's made it to the kitchen and through the backdoor that leads to the gardens. The stone patio is damp with dew. I listen for her ragged breathing, but she must be further away now.

"I'm going to find you," I shout into the night, taunting her.

I see her retreating figure in the small sliver of moonlight that peaks behind a dark cloud. She sprints toward the forest that lines the back of the property. Smart girl. I run faster, easily closing the distance she's made between us. She's maybe only a few seconds ahead now.

The forest stretches as far as I can see. The darkness swallows anything not within an arm's distance. I keep running. After a few minutes, I realize I'm no longer tracking her. I slow to a walk. There's no sound. No witnesses. An empty, secluded wood. The perfect escape. She really does have the advantage. *Fuck.* If she wants to leave me tonight, she will. And I suppose I'll have my answer.

Chapter Forty-One: Meghan

Run. It's the only thought I can complete. Run. I urge my legs on faster with every step. My thighs burn from the effort, but I don't stop. I'm not fast. Surely, he's right behind me. I have to run faster.

Instinct takes over, leaving little agency for doubt. My heart beats hard enough to push metallic-tinged air through my lungs. My feet don't hit the ground in a smooth rhythm. I stumble over tree roots hidden beneath leaves and damp earth. It's too dark to see where I'm going. Every step forward is a blind move of faith in between the trunks of trees. I swerve, jump, and try to make myself move faster, but as if in a dream, I don't feel my body speed up.

I'm not sure how long I've been running, but I know it's been long enough for him to catch me. Any minute, my legs scream, any minute, and he'll catch up. I won't make it. Any minute now, and he'll take me.

I run despite that. I run not even knowing whether or not I want to escape.

The trees start to thin out. The sounds of tires on wet pavement swish past, and I know I'm moving in the right direction. The road is ahead. Just a few more minutes, and I can make it to the road. The wooded area slopes downward the closer I get to the noise. I stumble over loose rock, but I catch myself before I can lose momentum. The only thing that stands between me and freedom is a small stream that edges the line between the Maddison property and the road.

All I need to do is jump. A small jump. It's maybe nine feet from one side to the other. The soft ground makes my footing uneven, but it won't take much to clear the water. The stream isn't deep, even if I don't. I could walk through it. I'm so close. Five more strides, and I'm there. Then two. But I hesitate. And the few seconds it takes me to slow near the water's edge is all it takes for Shane to catch me.

His body's heat envelopes me in the cool night. His arms wrap around my shoulders, trapping mine at my sides and draining the last bit of adrenaline that was carrying me forward. His muscles tighten around me when I struggle. The strength of his hold is almost suffocating, and I hate how relieved I am that he's won. That this is over.

It's warm in his embrace. Comforting to the point of drowsiness. Like a part of me knew I'd end up here all along. The excitement of the chase made all that more satisfying. Adrenaline drips out of my fingertips until my limbs fall slack.

"You're mine." His lips murmur against me. His arms release me, only for his hands to grip my shoulders then shove me against the nearest tree. He presses against me so hard that the side of my face is forced into the ragged bark. The pain ebbs into pleasure. I groan. The sound encourages him. One hand holds me in place. His thumb brushes the space between my shoulder blades as he uses the other to shuffle through something. I try to turn around and see what it is, but he presses the restraining hand into my back to prevent me from moving.

Before I can ask, Shane has my wrists in his hands. He keeps his knee against the back of mine while his fingers make quick work of the bindings. The final pull of the knot pinches my skin together.

"You are mine." He yanks me around, shoving my back and hands into the trunk.

It hurts. The angle creates sharp pressure along the bones of my hands.

"Say you're mine." His face lowers to my neck. He nips at me until goosebumps run down my skin. "Say it."

I don't respond. The strange mix of pain and pleasure short-circuits my thoughts before they can fully form.

"Maybe you didn't hear me." His voice echoes into the dark silence around us. "Let me help you focus." His hand grips my neck, keeping my chin up and my eyes on him. "Say you're mine."

"I'm yours." I swallow.

It's like we exhale the same breath. I don't know what this means, but I know I mean it. I couldn't help it, even if I wanted to. My heart belongs to Shane. And he'll make sure my body does as well.

He yanks me forward and pushes me to my knees. I stumble. It's hard to balance with my hands tied behind my back. It's not graceful, so it's certainly not sexy. But he doesn't seem to mind my clumsiness.

"You're so perfect," he whispers. "Do you know that?" His fingers linger for a moment on the button of his jeans. "So fucking perfect."

I watch as he slowly unzips his pants.

"Open," he says. He fists his dick inches from my lips.

My pussy clenches. I do as I'm told, looking up at him, determined to see the look on his face as I take his dick in my mouth.

He shoves it inside of me before I'm ready. I gag, but it doesn't stop him. He fucks my mouth like he's won and I'm the prize. I try my best to hallow my cheeks. I don't want to disappoint him. He thrusts in and out. I can't steady myself with my hands, so I lean my forehead into his body as he pushes himself into me. I love every bit of it. I love the way his hands grip my hair. The way he keeps me trapped for his pleasure. Every touch, every moment of intimacy so far, has been for me, and there's nothing I want more than to finally get the chance to do something for him.

I have to be good for him. I have to make him come. That's all I can think of. That, and trying not to gag. My jaw hurts from how wide I have to keep my lips open to stop my teeth from sliding against him. But I won't give in. Before I can really begin to enjoy how full he fills my mouth, he pulls out. Unfinished tears stream down my face as he shoves me to the ground.

"Good girl," he says. His hand presses my head into the forest floor.

My damp cheek sticks against the fallen leaves, but I'm too high on his praise to be bothered. He pulls my pants down with one hand as the other tangles in my hair and pulls back on my head.

"Such a good girl. You will always be mine." He pushes inside of me with ease. "You'll never escape me."

Chapter Forty-Two: Shane

I wrap my hand in her hair and yank her head back. She's so short. So easy to grab and move where I need. I want to see as much of that pretty little face as I can in the moonlight. I pull her face to the side so that I can watch the pleasure build. She squeezes her eyes tight as I slam into her harder. Her thighs tense and shake beneath me. I can feel she's close.

I pull her hair with each thrust. She cries out, and it nearly makes me come. I won't last long. I pump harder.

"Shane," she begs. "Please."

I love how my name sounds on her lips. I take my other hand and wrap it around her neck. In response, she arches her back even more. She doesn't shy away from the onslaught. She puts herself into it. And I know I can't hold off any longer.

"Shane. I'm yours," she cries. "Oh god, I'm yours."

I pull out of her fast and finish all over her back. I cover her body, loving how much I dominate her. She's more beautiful all the time. It's fucking insane. More beautiful in my clothes. More beautiful in my bed. More beautiful with my cum all over her perfect skin.

I take her back to our room. She lost, so she won't get a say tonight. She's too spent to fight back anyway. It makes me hard again.

I wonder if I'll ever get enough.

I untie her wrists only to tie her to the bed. I position her so her legs are splayed open, her arms outstretched. I kiss her forehead, her nose, then her lips. Then I place the gag around her soft mouth. And the blindfold around her eyes.

"You can't do anything, little siren. You're mine. Forever. You're completely at my mercy."

I make her come. Over and over again. Until the tears fall down her cheeks as her body shakes.

Then I fuck her one more time. And we come together.

CHAPTER FORTY-THREE: MEGHAN

My wrists are sore, so I rub the skin. I allowed myself to be captured. I let him trap me, tie me up. I relished every second of it. I knew what it would cost me.

It's still dark when I wake. Shane is asleep, but I can't wait any longer. I need coffee. I need to think. I've made some kind of decision, and I'm not entirely sure why. I took the ring. That's one thing. I wanted the success I've deserved. I wanted the safety it would provide. But then I allowed myself to be caught. I stopped short of freedom. I chose not to escape. Even though I knew what that would mean to Shane and what that might mean for us.

My heart aches. I've given every piece of myself away to a man without understanding what parts he even wants to keep.

I find some of Shane's clothes to wear and tie my hair back in a ponytail to hide the mess he made of me last night. My hair is tangled from root to end. I can still feel his fingers tug against my scalp, his smell still wrapped around my neck like his hands never left my body. I shake my head to erase the memories. I can't think when my mind is still strangled by his overwhelming presence.

I shut the door behind me with a soft click and hurry down the hall. Each step clears the edges around my thoughts, and fresh air helps lessen the tightness in my chest. The house is quiet. I'm relieved at the time away to just be with myself. I make it to the stairway landing without as much as a creak from a floorboard.

The kitchen is empty, but my instincts were right, people this rich have an espresso machine. I pull two cups down from the cabinet and make us coffee. I watch the espresso layer in the glass as it pours. The beautiful brown ombre reminds me of Shane's eyes. The way the soft color turns dark with desire every time he touches me.

My mind replays last night despite my best attempts. I shiver. The moment I think of him, I can feel the pressure of his touch against my skin once more. Smell his cologne on my clothes. Taste his kiss on my lips. As if my body is reminding me to beg me for more.

Fuck. I shift my weight back and forth as I watch the espresso finish pulling. Every piece of this man has dug a home beneath the shell of my heart and into my soul. Of course I let him catch me. I was naive for thinking I would want anything else. He's everything I've ever wanted. I'm an addict. And he's made me realize love is the most consuming drug. I just hope this time I'm not trading one poison for another.

I find cream in the fridge for his and ice for mine. I'm about to round the corner when Elise stops me.

"Oh, er . . . good morning," I say. I try to keep my voice bright and kind. We didn't spend much time with his family. I'm not sure what to make of his stepmother.

"Mmm." It's all the greeting Elise offers. She shuffles around me as if she doesn't plan on saying more.

I'm about to turn and leave again when her voice stops me.

"You know, you're not quite his . . . type."

"I'm sorry?" I turn around to look at her mouth. I've clearly heard her words wrong, so maybe my hearing has gone bad.

"You're not his type." The words are stronger. Elise smiles, but the gesture is cold. She looks me up and down.

I'm not going to admit my insecurities to this woman. "I'm sorry you know your stepson so little that you would think that way. But I love him. And he loves me." I say the words to hurt Elise and end up hurting myself. It's the first time I've admitted I love Shane, and now that I've said the words, I'm afraid they're true.

I'm in love with Shane.

I don't know if I want to be in love, but I know I want more.

A hot, sickly nausea claws its way up from my stomach and into my throat.

Her thin lips fall. "He'll never truly love you, you know. Take it from me, he's just like his father."

"You know, that might be true, Elise. But the difference between you and me is that I do love him. And that makes this worth the effort. Even if it doesn't end in my favor."

CHAPTER FORTY-FOUR: SHANE

The white tent on the grounds at the back of the estate has been transformed in hours. Gone is the plastic piping that ran from one end to the other. Now, the ceiling is dripping with soft white flowers with delicate greenery. Small lights are woven into the arrangement, making the room feel more like a fairy garden than the backyard of my parents' home.

I can't say this is my vision of happily-ever-after. The extravagant floral display, four-piece quartet, and three-course dinner surely cost enough to buy Meghan a *Chanel* bag in every color. If it were me, if it was us, I'd rather just elope. Spend the money on the most extravagant honeymoon and treat her like the queen she is.

I look over at her. I don't think I've ever imagined a future like I have with her. Then again, I've never met a person like her. I'd marry her just like this. The idea takes hold in my imagination. She's fucking breathtaking. Her long auburn hair is swept up in a clip, showing off the slope of her shoulders, the neckline on her green dress delicately displaying her cleavage. We could make tonight the start of our honeymoon. I want to reach over and drag her lips to mine, but at last second, I hesitate.

Something feels off. Meghan shifts side to side in her seat with pent-up energy. She seems anxious. I try to rationalize it. I tell myself it's because of my nerves, not her behavior. The daydreaming has me worried about a future I haven't even started. I can't be convinced she wants to say no when I haven't even asked.

The immediate family is the first to arrive. They fill in the seats around us at the long table near what will transform into the dance floor tomorrow. Although tonight is just the rehearsal dinner, I watch Elise pace back and forth around the centerpieces, adjusting and straightening arrangements as if someone might measure the distance between each rose petal.

Carson stands. "Please, if we can have everyone seated, we're going to begin practicing the processional." He says the statement in general, but he waves specifically to our mother to sit down. She doesn't listen. He clears his throat and goes on. "Okay, then. If we can have the groomsmen line up."

Carson's friends are the same variation of former football player turned fraternity brother who managed to get accepted into law school. They might be in their twenties, but it wouldn't be obvious from the way they push and shove each other as if this was another Friday night out.

Abbey's bridesmaids are actually much the same. It's almost as if all rich kids with rich families and rich grandparents inherit the same personality traits along with their trust funds. It makes me feel better about my decision to drop out and join the Army while trying to find my own path. Father won't let me run the family business now, but at least I can say I made it on my own. Or at least, I tried more than the rest.

"Why aren't you up there?" Meghan leans into me to whisper. She smells so good I want to wrap myself around her until she's all I breathe. I hold her hand instead.

"I wasn't even invited," I say.

Each member of the wedding party finds their other pair. They line up at the end of the aisle, arms intertwined at the elbow, and practice walking in measured steps in time with the music. Abbey and Carson have gone with the traditional wedding march. A tune as unoriginal as the theme of the day.

"Why? If you don't mind me asking." Meghan asks, eventually. She bites her lip as she looks up at me. I know it's out of nervousness and care for my tenuous relationship with my family, but immediately my attention turns to more intimate ideas. We don't have to stay for the entire rehearsal dinner. We can slip away sometime between courses.

"This isn't really my kind of thing," I say. I run my fingertips up and down her thigh, inching my touch inward with each stroke.

"Weddings?" Her forehead scrunches. She sounds upset. I'm surprised. I understand she's a romantic, obviously. But I didn't know if that included marriage. I suppose I wouldn't care either way since she's mine.

"These kinds of weddings," I stress the first word so she understands. "I'm not a big fan of the traditional." I smile.

"Oh, I've noticed," she snaps, but I can tell it's playful now. She leans into me.

The wedding party finishes practicing, and everyone takes their seats. The movement is enough of a distraction for me to slip my fingers beneath the hem of Meghan's dress. I know she feels the excitement I do when I hear her sharp intake of breath and see her chest rise and fall in time with my determination. She's not wearing any underwear. Her thighs are already wet with desire. I push apart her legs and stroke her soft skin, easing my fingers up and down before circling her clit. I'm going to bring her to the edge and see what she does. I want to see how long it takes to hear her sweet voice beg again.

My father stands and interrupts what I want to do next. He clinks his knife against his glass. It's unnecessary as a hush rolls over the tent the moment he stands. He clears his throat, raising his glass. "To the happy couple."

The crowd repeats. I slow my rhythm. All eyes of the dinner are upon our table. Our seats. I'm seated next to my father, and as badly as I'd like to make Meghan blush, her pleasure is for me and me alone. She lets out a strangled whimper as I remove my fingers from her clit. She's going to learn patience today.

"We're here today to celebrate the love of Carson and Abbey," my father says.

Everyone applauds politely. I keep my hand between her thighs.

"But I'd also like to seize this opportunity to make another announcement."

The first person I look for is Carson. Surely my father isn't about to announce their pregnancy. It's too early. Too scandalous for conservative Elise and her conservative country club friends. But Carson looks just as confused as I am. I look to Elise next. If anyone is going to upstage her baby boy's day, surely they have her approval. But Elise's gaze narrows upon my father.

He continues on as if he can't feel Elise's stare. "Tonight, we celebrate the marriage of my youngest son, Carson." His hand clasps his shoulder. "And the engagement of my other." His right hand lands on mine. "To the happy marriages of both of my boys. I'm so proud."

Marriage. Both my boys. The words repeat in my head without meaning. It takes me several breaths to understand he said this out loud. I challenged him by taking Meghan without a plan and then risked it all for my ego by showing her off at this stupid wedding. This is my punishment. He's going to force me to marry someone else. In front of her. I squeeze her leg so she doesn't worry, even as my tongue tastes metallic with nerves. I won't do it. I won't lose her. I don't care what I have to do. He can't make me give her up.

Elise glares at me the way I wish to look at my father, as if hoping a gaze alone will cause someone to catch fire. I don't want to give her the satisfaction of my confusion or him the victory of my fear. I stay still. My grasp on Meghan is so tight now that even if they tried to physically tear her away from me, they'd fail.

"Please, don't keep us in suspense," Elise croons. "Who's the lucky woman."

I could beat my father to it. Announce my plans to marry Meghan in front of everyone before my father can try to break us apart. Elise sneers as if sensing my panic. She knows I didn't ask Meghan to marry me. It pisses me off. I can see it on her smug face. She thinks Meghan doesn't mean what I've claimed. And clearly my father thinks he knows what's best for me. As if I'm still a boy he can manipulate.

They think Meghan's just another political pawn they can scare off. That I won't fight to keep her. But they're wrong. I never thought of marriage because I never imagined finding a person worth spending forever with. Now I can't imagine spending a day apart.

I should've bought her a ring before bringing her here. It would've made the public display of my claim on her more politically correct. More secure. I don't like the idea that my mother will make her feel less than and my father will try to prevent it from happening. Poor Meghan, she's probably sick at the thought that I've used her while promised to another. I don't know how I'll convince her that it's all a lie. I look over to tell her something, anything to make her forgive me.

I steel myself for her terror. I create small variations of plans that will protect her and convince her of my love. Because I do love her. She needs to know she's not a game to me. Not now, not ever. Not even in the beginning.

And then Meghan smiles. Smiles.

She squeezes my hand on her thigh and places her left hand on the table. Everyone gasps, including me. Then she stands, smoothing the bottom of her dress, and shows off the ring to those too far away to see. The hushed whispers of uncertainty break into applause. Meghan beams at the crowd, then at me. I nearly choke as I try to swallow a steadying breath.

My father wants me to marry Meghan. I run my hand over my face as the realization strikes me. This was never about a corporate acquisition. It was always about Meghan. He wanted Meghan. For what I can't yet figure out, but I will. And I sure as fuck will marry her.

I blink to make sure I'm not hallucinating. Surely there's no way she's excited to be tied to me forever. I couldn't be that lucky. But Meghan's face lights up as if it's her game we've played together all along.

I look over to my father. He raises his glass to me and winks. Of course. He got to her somehow. But the jokes on him. I stand beside my future bride, take her hand in mine, and squeeze. I won. I was never going to let her go. This just buys me more time to convince her she always belonged with me.

The large, emerald-cut two-carat ring sits perfectly on her finger. A diamond that big always looked as if it would overpower the wearer. Grandma Maddison died before I was born. I never met her. Never saw it on anyone. Always wondered who my brother would marry that my father would deem worthy enough to wear it. When he didn't offer it to Carson, I understood. Abbey isn't the type of person who can wear that ring.

But now I know Meghan is.

It's hard to remain seated for the rest of the dinner. I want to take my future bride anywhere but here. I want to whisk her away before someone can take this dream from me. Secure our marriage then demand an explanation from my father.

It seems neither of those options is possible.

I put my hand back on her thigh. I'd sooner die than let her out of my sight now. I wonder how she's feeling. I choose to think she's as excited as me. I can't quite see her face. I brush a strand of hair behind her ear and trace my fingers down the curve of her neck. She moans softly and leans closer. I fixate on her body's response to me and shove down the questions of why and how she agreed to make such an announcement when clearly my father put her up to this.

My father. I can't get to him without making a scene and placing Meghan into uncomfortable scrutiny. Every time I look over to speak to my father, he finds a way to slip away. The bastard is still playing games. Getting off on every moment of my frustration.

"Let's go back to our room," I whisper into Meghan's ear. I place small kisses along the side of her throat to encourage the right response.

"S-sure," she says, breathless already.

I'm going to fuck her until she cries. As soon as I have my answers, I won't leave her side again. Meghan and I leave hand in hand, smiling and thanking the well-wishers as we move away from the grounds back to the estate. I want nothing more than to disappear into the dark with my future wife, but I know there's a lot to be done tonight before that sort of relaxation becomes possible.

I'm careful to take my time with her body. I never want to make her feel rushed. Each kiss, each lap of my tongue carries the love I feel for her. Every touch, every caress is an opportunity to prove to her just how deeply I mean the words I've said.

Only when her legs shake and she pleads for me to stop do I let her thighs drop from around my face. Normally, I would want to keep going, but tonight, she deserves to rest. I kiss my way down her legs and ease myself off of the comforter so I can tuck her body in tight. I lie next to her, stroking her head until her breathing evens out and she falls asleep. I wait a few minutes more to make sure she's asleep before I slip away.

My father is ready for me. If I expected him to be combative, I was sorely mistaken. In my mind, he always wanted to control me. When I ran away from our family, from his plan, I thought he finally understood I would never be the son he wanted. Instead, it was me who got it wrong. I've clearly become exactly the man he hoped for.

I don't bother knocking on his door, but he's waiting for me anyway. The office is more organized than usual. The papers that normally tower on his desk are gone. I can't imagine they're filed away. Clients don't just fit neatly into storage. Their business is ongoing. Thomas is cruel but brilliant. The more he has going on, the more successful his outcomes seem to be. This is the office of someone normal. Someone who takes days off and perhaps spends time with their family.

"What do you want?" I ask.

"I let the right woman get away," he says as a form of greeting.

I close the door behind me.

Thomas sits in his chair, shifting back and forth slightly. He doesn't look at me.

"And I hurt another because of it." He swirls the short glass in his hand. "Your mother was the love of my life, and Elise never forgave me for it." He hangs his head.

For the first time in my life, my father looks remorseful. The wrinkles around his face seem deeper than usual. The hollowness to his skin causing him to look stretched and tired.

"I kept her prisoner to this life I created, and I regret it every day. But regardless of her flaws, I knew she would be a mother to you boys, and I did what I had to do to keep the family we had together. I spent the rest of my life trying to make it up to her, and a part of me thinks this cancer is what I get as my punishment." Silence. "You never wanted my advice, not even as a boy. So follow my directive instead. Marry Meghan. Inherit what I've built. And make amends to those I couldn't." He pushes himself back from his desk and walks to the fireplace.

"Why didn't you tell me?" I ask.

"Would you have listened if I did?" He chuckles as he shoves his hands in his pockets when he turns to look at the fire.

"I don't know, maybe." It's a lie. We both know it.

"It's never a son's responsibility to listen to his father. It's up to the father to find a way to make his son listen."

"Dad, I, I don't—" I start to say, but he cuts me.

"Don't hate Elise. She's the only mother you knew. And considering what I've done to her, that's more than I could've hoped for. Don't take it out on her. She put that clause in the will to punish me, not you. She never imagined you'd marry, so she assumed that the inheritance would go to Carson as a result." He turns around to face me, and he smiles, but it doesn't reach his eyes. "And if you still hate her, then let me have this last win. But if you hate me, do it for Meghan. Cherish her because I couldn't cherish the woman I loved. And it will always be my biggest regret."

"She doesn't want to marry me," I say. The words hurt, as if they take all the air from my lungs as they leave my mouth. It's too great a fear to shove back inside.

"I've never known you to give up so easily."

"This isn't a game I can win. This is her life." I can't force her to love me. This is something she has to choose.

"I see the way she looks at you."

"Her attraction to me isn't enough to stay." It pains me to say it aloud. I can't fuck my way into her heart. No matter how hard I've tried.

My father considers me for a moment. It's the longest we've been alone together since I was a child.

"Then become the man she can't afford to lose." He clasps me on the shoulder before walking out of the room.

Chapter Forty-Five: Meghan

I wake up around midnight because I'm too warm with my head resting against Shane's chest and a thigh wrapped around his legs. He's awake still. He has one arm draped around my shoulder, his hand stroking my back, while he uses the other hand to scroll through his emails.

I kick the duvet off of my legs to free my skin from the heat.

"Bad dream?" he asks. He sets down his phone to tuck my hair behind my ear.

"Hungry," I say as I sit up.

Shane is so handsome, even in this light. I smile. He's mine. Somehow, this might all work out. The career. The husband. Somehow, I might have it all.

"You know, I think I could go for something sweet, now that you mention it." He laughs as he pins me beneath him and kisses his way down my stomach to my thighs.

"No," I squeal. I wiggle beneath his tender caress of my skin. "Food. Real food." I slip my fingers into his hair and yank playfully on the long strands.

"Ugh," he groans, sitting back to give me space. "Fine. I suppose I could settle for something chocolate. What can I get you?"

"No, no, I can do it. Do you think there's ice cream in the kitchen?"

"Yeah, of course. Stay here. Let me do it."

"No. I think you've earned it. Let me take care of you."

I slip out of the bed before he can stop me. I throw on his clothes from the floor again and hurry down the hall as if he might chase me. My pulse races as I realize I'd like nothing more than him to chase me down the steps and tie me up while he feeds me chocolate and fucks me.

Sex has never been the hard part for us. I told Shane I'd get the dessert to buy myself some time to figure out how to tell him how I feel. I knew it the second I woke up. I can't wait any longer. I have to tell him I love him. I just don't know how yet.

But I never get time to myself in this house. Elise is sitting at the island, her blonde hair is slicked back in a tight bun. She's reading something on her *iPad*. Her glasses slip down her nose, and she pushes them up before taking a sip of wine. As the glass meets her lips, she must realize I'm there because she makes a disapproving tsk and shuts the cover on her tablet case.

Any hope I had that this time she'd keep quiet quickly disappears.

"Congratulations on your nuptials," she says.

"Thank you," I say. I can tell she doesn't mean it.

"You're agreeing to be one of many. Forgive me if I don't attend this mockery of marriage."

I twist the band on the underside of my finger for comfort. I don't bother to respond.

"I hope you understand you're setting yourself up for a lifetime of nauseous suspicions and anxious nights in an empty bed."

Is that what she's doing now? I wonder. I walk around the island. I can see the red beneath her eyes. The hollowness of her face that only comes from crying too much for too long. I feel sorry for Elise. This is clearly not the life she pictured. Not the love she dreamed for herself. I imagine what that must feel like, to remember walking down an aisle to a man who would never love you the way that you deserved to be loved. The way it would feel every anniversary, to watch him grow more distant, all while unable to pinpoint the moment you went wrong.

"I hope, Elise." I take out two spoons and close the drawer with a smooth thud. "That I never have to live those moments. Every person deserves to be loved the way they want. Even you, even now." I offer her a tight smile but don't wait for her response. I walk to the freezer, grab the first container of ice cream I see, and leave.

My heart hammers in my chest as I walk up the stairs. I'm out of breath by the time I reach the landing, not out of physical effort, but rather mental strain. I meant what I said. I can't imagine being married to a man that doesn't love me. I won't make the same mistake.

I walk into the room.

Shane grabs the ice cream container and tosses it on the bed so he can wrap me in his body.

"Don't, Shane," I say as he pulls me into him. I shouldn't have expected less. He's not normal. He's always trying to have more of me.

"I love it when you say my name. Say it again," he murmurs.

"Please, don't." I slap his hand away. Love. Oh god. I was always going to have to tell him. I make my voice stern so he understands I'm not playing hard to get. This time, I mean it. We were always going to have to have this conversation. It might as well be tonight.

The playful gleam that softness his cheeks falls slack. His brows pinch together in realization. And that realization turns to cold rage.

"Don't you get it? I'll never stop, Meghan. You're my siren. And I've heard your song. I'll follow it forever or die trying to get back to you."

"You can't mean that," I say. Yet every piece of me hopes somehow he does. Because maybe then, he could love me, too.

"I've never meant anything more."

I shake my head. "That doesn't mean you can just have me. I don't belong to you. Even if you think you belong with me." I twist the ring on my finger. Suddenly it feels too heavy.

"It's too late. I've agreed. And so have you."

"I didn't agree to anything because I was never really given a choice! Doesn't what I want matter to you at all? Shouldn't the woman you supposedly love be allowed to make her own decisions?" He should be just as mad as I am. He shouldn't want to marry someone who was tricked into it. I could leave him. I could hurt him. None of this is real. I was so stupid to think it could be real.

"Oh, but you did. You made your decision when you didn't try to escape. You reaffirmed your decision when you let me catch you. You sealed your fate when you accepted that ring." He steps closer to me. "But we can keep pretending if it makes you feel better. I know you find pleasure in me taking away your will."

"I'll never love you," I say. Another lie. I've become a liar.

"I don't need your love," he says.

"Then what do you even want me for?" I yell. I'm tired. I'm tired of being a pawn in his game that I don't know the rules. I'm tired of not mattering to the people in my life. I'm tired of being used.

"Your life," he says simply.

"You're sick."

"And you like it. No, even better, I'm exactly what you think you deserve. But that's the best part." He towers over me. "I'm no Prince Charming, but I'll give you everything you're too ashamed, too afraid to want, and it'll be better than anything you've ever imagined. And in exchange" — he runs his knuckles over my cheek — "you'll spend the rest of your life with me. So I don't have to search any longer for the special kind of peace you provide."

"I don't like this," I say. I step away to create space between us. I can never think straight when he's close.

"What don't you like?" He sounds frustrated again.

"I don't like any of it, Shane!" I throw my hands into the air. "I don't like the idea of getting married just to get divorced. I don't like the idea of getting married forever, a forever of you shoving my face down into things so that you don't have to look at me and see a woman you never loved. I don't like the idea of having to be tied up just for you to get off. I don't like the idea of constantly being reminded that I'm not enough just the way I am. When we're together, when we're intimate, when we celebrate anniversaries, always knowing in the back of my head that none of this was ever real." I let the tears fall down my face without shame. "It's too much to ask."

"Is that what you think this is?" His chest heaves with emotion that rivals my own. "After everything I've told you? You think I'm asking to reduce your spirit, shape you into something docile, and make you an object I use to discard?" He runs a hand through his hair.

"Is that not what you're doing?" I challenge. I straighten my shoulders to look him in the eyes better.

"What part of my offer made you think that?"

"Elise said," I begin. And it's the wrong thing to say. Because he pounces. Backing me into the wall and pressing his body into mine.

His fingers grasp my chin, holding me in place. The touch is gentle, but firm, his thumb caressing my lips before he speaks. "Your face is most beautiful in my hands. Where I can hold you still and watch every second of pleasure that I ring from your body."

I can feel the truth in his words from the growing erection that presses into my stomach.

"I like the idea of having you tied up so I can get you off as many times as I like. I like the idea that you intoxicate me so much that I have to have you whenever I wish. Not to discard, Meghan. To worship. To help shape you into whatever you want to be. And to explore any desire you might have."

I want to argue, but he continues on.

"Elise is a cunt who wouldn't know love if it sat at one of her fancy dinner parties in front of a nameplate. But you're not wrong about everything." He stresses the last sentence. "I do want to use your body. I've never wanted anything more. Do you know what it's like? To not be able to come without picturing your pretty little face."

His fingers grip me harder until tears prick in my eyes, but I can't help the moan that escapes my lips.

"Do you know what it's like to be a grown man and have to sneak away to jerk off at work because the woman I just met brushed her body against mine? That within days of meeting you, I couldn't think of anything else? Because you looked up at me beneath those frustrating, beautiful eyes, I became so obsessed that just the smell of your perfume makes me hard. And now that I've had you, been inside of you, you think I could leave?" He laughs. "I agreed to this marriage because it's a start. But I'll admit, vows won't be enough for me. Mark my words, I'll find a way to keep you longer than *'till death do us part.*"

"You can't mean that." I hiccup.

"I do. I don't care if you don't yet because I know you will."

"But if you just love me for my body, then—" He doesn't let me finish the thought.

"I love you for your body, for your words, for the way you fight back, physically, verbally. I love the way you look up at me, the way you feel in my arms as you fall asleep against my chest. I love that you're difficult, and particular, and stubborn as hell. I love that you're unapologetic for the things you believe in and that you're brave and fearless when fighting for others. And I love that you're a paradox. That you're shy and embarrassed easily and that you look at me for comfort and validation, even when you hate me. I love everything about you. Your flaws and your flawlessness. You're perfect, Meghan. Not because someone needs to be perfect, but because you're you. And I wouldn't have anyone else. I love you."

The tears fall fast as I bury my face below his chest, and his arms wrap around my back. "I love you, too."

He strokes my hair in between kisses as I cry out all the fear I've felt these last few days, the last few years. I've been hurt so many times I was convinced I'd never love again. Certain I'd never feel something unconditional, passionate, yet safe. Then Shane showed up and took away that doubt. Now I know this isn't just make-believe, he means every word he says.

Chapter Forty-Six: Meghan

The next morning is the day of the wedding.

Our wedding.

I dress quickly. I'm really getting married. Oh god, I don't want to overthink it. I put on my favorite of the dresses Shane's bought me. A black satin bodice with a sweet tulle skirt. I laugh to myself. I hope we can take pictures. My parents will die at the world finding out their daughter eloped in a black wedding dress.

Shane walks out of the bathroom.

"You're not supposed to see me!" I cry.

"I'm not supposed to do a lot of things," he says. He takes my hand. "But I don't believe in luck. I do believe in soulmates, however." He spins me around so my back is trapped against his chest. He kisses my neck slowly, and I arch into him.

"Shane." I moan. "You're not supposed to seduce the bride before the wedding."

"I just wanted to remind you why you have to say yes," he murmurs into my skin. "And to tell you I love you."

"I'm going to say yes." I roll my eyes. I've come this far. I'm not backing out now. "And I love you, too."

"Good. Close your eyes."

"Shane, we're gonna be late to our own vows." But I do as I'm told. It's not like we've saved ourselves for marriage. Sex right before the wedding can't make this any less traditional than we already are.

Instead of feeling his hand tighten around my skin or

feeling him press his hard length into my back, I feel a delicate chain set around my shoulder, then a weight drops against my hip.

"Open your eyes," he says. He directs me toward the mirror.

I touch the weight hanging from my arm. "It's beautiful." The delicate gold hardware is woven into the soft pink leather. Tears burn my eyes, and I have to blink away the image. My pink *Chanel* bag.

"Just like you."

"Shane." I turn around to face him. "I don't, you didn't have to, I didn't win. You didn't beg."

"Well." He smoothes the hair near my face and tucks the loose strands behind my ear. "I didn't have to buy you a ring." He holds my hand up and kisses my diamond. "I didn't buy you a proper wedding dress. I didn't buy you a bouquet. I'd hate for you to walk down the aisle thinking I didn't love you." He kisses my forehead. "Do you love it?"

"I do . . . but how did you buy it?"

"I bought it right after you said you wanted it. When we were fighting."

"But you couldn't know what was about to happen?" I lean into his chest.

"No." He kisses my head and strokes my hair. "But I always knew I'd give you anything you've ever wanted."

"You already have."

"And that's how it will be for the rest of our lives."

CHAPTER FORTY-SEVEN: SHANE

Rain falls in a steady rhythm against the concrete patio, filling in the beige with gray. The pale pink peonies stand out brightly against the dull morning sky.

My bride walks down the aisle. Her black dress flows behind her as the wind brushes against the tulle bottom, making her look like the dark goddess of my dreams.

Our vows aren't traditional. I made sure the judge wouldn't waste our time with nonsense about God blessing this union. There is no blessing. My actions made this happen. And *she* is my god. And the only vow I'll make today is to worship her until she believes it. Meghan doesn't need my protection, but she'll have it. She doesn't need my money, but I'll spoil her anyway. And in sickness and in health only applies to her because when she dies, I'm certain I will, too.

I stand in front of her, fully aware that this woman is now my life as much as the heart that beats in my chest.

Her tiny hands shake in mine. She bites her lip as she looks up at me. I see nerves in the tears welling behind her glasses.

I kiss her head. "I will honor and cherish you, Meghan. Forever." I whisper the words, and her shoulders drop as I squeeze her tighter.

"Do you, Shane, take Meghan to be your wife?" the judge asks as she turns to me.

"I do," I say.

"Do you, Meghan, take Shane to be your husband?"

"I do," she says.

I wrap my arms around her and pull her into my chest. One

hand encases her body while the other tangles in her hair. And I kiss my wife.

The End.

About the Author

Arabella Ames is a romance author and cat mom, who spends her days drinking espresso and falling in love with a new version of the same morally gray man. She has her MFA in fiction writing, and enjoys traveling, mountain climbing, and consuming novels.